Ignacio

Delaney Diamond

Garden Avenue Press

Ignacio by Delaney Diamond

Garden Avenue Press

Atlanta, Georgia

978-1-946302-87-8 (Ebook edition)

978-1-946302-88-5 (Paperback edition)

www.delaneydiamond.com

Chapter One

Ignacio rolled over, squinting against the sun's glare coming in through the bedroom window. He'd thrown one of his famous parties last night and then fell into bed after everyone had left.

What time is it? he wondered.

He scraped his phone off the table beside him and saw it was almost noon. Wonderful. Half the day was already gone.

Groaning, he rolled his naked body from under the tangled sheets, frowning when a white lace bra fell to the hardwood floor from beneath the folds. Who did *that* belong to? His foggy brain couldn't remember sleeping with anyone the night before, but whoever she was, she was long gone because he was alone.

Ignacio tugged on a pair of red boxer briefs he picked up from the floor and staggered toward the open door. Quietly yawning, he shoved his fingers through his long, rumpled hair and pushed it back from his face.

Pausing in the doorway, he surveyed the disarray of his living room. With the blinds open, the oversized windows displayed blue skies and the Los Angeles skyline, a sharp contrast to the carnage from the night before.

He wrinkled his nose against the scent of stale alcohol and leftover food. An empty bottle of rum lay on its side, the contents spilled onto the white rug beneath the table it rested on. Plates and bowls with half-eaten snacks were scattered around the room, and broken glass was strewn across the wooden floor where a goblet of white wine had fallen off the nearby bookcase.

Empty beer bottles caught the sunlight and glinted at him from various surfaces. Several articles of clothing had been left behind too, including a jacket he didn't recognize—definitely not his—and a pink and gold stiletto abandoned in the corner. Did the owner leave with only one shoe?

Shaking his head, Ignacio muttered a Spanish curse. The place was such a mess, there was no way he was going to clean it all by himself. He'd have his assistant call a service.

He righted an overturned chair, vaguely remembering one of his actor friends, Vincent, had tossed it aside in a moment of drunken exuberance. He shook his head, laughing softly. Typical Vincent.

A faint buzzing caught his attention as a phone vibrated somewhere in the room. Following the sound, he found the device tucked between the sofa cushions.

"That's mine."

Ignacio straightened with a start at the sound of the voice. *What the...?*

A woman walked in from the direction of his bathroom. Her blonde hair, parted in the middle, was slicked back into a ponytail. Cosmetically enhanced lips smiled at him as she extended a hand. Ignacio placed the phone on her open palm.

"I had a great time last night," she said, tucking the phone into the small purse on her wrist. "Call me if you want to get together again." She kissed his cheek and then strutted toward the door.

Ignacio stared after her. Did the bra belong to her?

"I need coffee," he muttered, ambling toward the kitchen and rubbing his hands down his face to wake up.

A few years ago, he had purchased a commercial-grade espresso machine and placed one in each of his homes, considering the equipment one of the best investments he had ever made. After he ground the beans, he made himself an espresso, letting out a satisfied moan as the warm liquid flowed down his throat.

He opened the cabinet and took down his pack of cigarettes, paused, and then grimaced before placing them back on the shelf. He was trying to quit—again.

"Mind over matter," he muttered to himself. If he was smart, he would remove them from his home completely, but he hadn't quite gotten there yet.

Ringing came from the bedroom, where he had left his phone. He hurried back there and answered when he saw his manager's name on the screen—Yvonne Williams.

"Good morning, Yvonne."

"Hello, Ignacio. How are you this morning?"

"Do you really want to know?" he asked, padding into the kitchen to grab his coffee.

"I wouldn't have asked if I didn't."

Yvonne acted more like a mother than the typical cutthroat manager. Probably because they had been working together since he was a teenager and she hadn't started out in the industry. For years, she had worked as a camp counselor, and perhaps for that reason was very protective of her young clients. She had treated Ignacio like one of her kids, filling him up with slices of the delicious sweet potato pies she brought into the office to share with the staff.

Back then, he had been trying to get his big break in Hollywood while trying to avoid special treatment as Benicio Santana's son, the legendary actor-director-producer from Mexico whose success in English-speaking films had been almost as celebrated as his career in Latin America.

"I feel as if a truck ran over me, backed up, and then ran over me again." Ignacio opened the sliding glass door and stepped onto the balcony.

Yvonne laughed. "Sounds like you had one of your famous parties again."

"I did," he admitted.

"You don't sound like you enjoyed yourself."

His reply was a noncommittal grunt. If he were being honest, the parties no longer brought him as much joy as they used to. He loved dancing and spending time with friends, but trashing his home in the name of a good time didn't seem like the best idea.

"I think I'll have to move these parties to another location in the future. Rent a club or something." Sitting in one of his chairs, he lifted his feet onto the metal railing and crossed them at the ankles. "What's up?"

"I have somewhat good news about your indie film."

His heart jumped. "Go ahead," he said, sipping his coffee.

His last foray into filmmaking hadn't gone very well. The film flopped, and he wasn't the only person who had lost money. His father had invested in the project along with a few other people. With a failure under his belt, he'd had a hard time convincing anyone that his latest project was worth the risk. He didn't want to ask his father again, and though he could probably convince his siblings to loan him the money, he wanted to finance the project himself, the way any indie filmmaker would, by finding his own backers.

"I assume you've only just gotten up for the day?" Yvonne asked.

"Yes."

"So you haven't seen the news, but you will eventually. There's a ton of publicity surrounding your meeting with Delta yesterday."

At the mention of his ex's name, the hairs rose on his skin, and his body stiffened. Earlier in the evening, before throwing the party, he had attended an event where Delta had also been present.

"I didn't have a meeting with her," he said coolly.

"Well, whatever you want to call it: a run-in, a get-together—"

"We happened to be in the same place at the same time. That's it."

"Honey, listen to me. It doesn't matter. A picture of the two of you together has gone viral and broken the internet, as the young people say. It's a PR boon—for both you and Delta."

"What are you talking about?"

"The world is excited by the idea of the two of you reconciling," Yvonne explained, as if the answer was obvious.

"*Reconciling?*" Ignacio dropped his feet to the concrete slab beneath him. Yvonne was going too far. "We exchanged a sentence and then went on our way. We haven't been a couple since I was twenty-one years old, when we were practically kids."

Their breakup was as fresh as if it had happened the day before. He would never admit it, but the pain of Delta's rejection had lingered for years.

"Ignacio," Yvonne said, using her motherly voice, which she always pulled out whenever she wanted to convince him to go along with one of her ideas. "This is the opportunity you've been waiting for. Maybe not exactly how you wanted it, but it's free publicity, honey, and almost every article or post I've seen mentions your movie. Folks are excited by the thought of two young lovers reuniting after all these years. It's the kind of thing movies are made of. A real-life love story."

"We're not back together, Yvonne," Ignacio said evenly. She must be hard of hearing.

"I know that. You know that. But the rest of the world doesn't."

"What are you saying?"

A brief pause. "Delta's people reached out to me."

"You mean her father," Ignacio said, the left side of his lip curling up in displeasure.

"Yes, Delta's father and her publicist. The publicity has been great for her too. Her music has seen a huge spike on the streaming platforms. They want to take full advantage of this opportunity."

Delta's parents had controlled her career since she blew judges away on a televised talent competition when she was ten years old, belting out the lyrics to "At Last" in a remarkably soulful voice for her age. Her father, especially, who was her manager, must be salivating at the thought of her songs climbing back up the charts.

"What are you not telling me, Yvonne?"

"Keep an open mind," she said carefully.

"About what?" he asked through gritted teeth.

"Delta and her father are still in L.A. and want to meet with you—about pretending you're back together to capitalize on the media frenzy. It was Eddie's idea, and I think it's brilliant."

To resist the urge to hurl his cup off the balcony, Ignacio carefully placed it on the table. "No."

"Ignacio, listen to me. This opportunity—"

"I will find backers for the movie without stooping to lying to the public."

"Or you could take a few publicity shots now and then with your ex."

"She's an ex for a reason."

Yvonne's voice softened. "Honey, I know she broke your heart, but that was ages ago. Don't cut off your nose to spite your face."

Ignacio stiffened. "She didn't break my heart," he all but snarled. Then he briefly closed his eyes.

He couldn't do it. He couldn't pretend for the cameras and handle the scrutiny that would inevitably come when the world thought they were back together. He could only imagine the barrage of questions about how and why they decided to give "love" another chance.

"Fine, she didn't break your heart, but you broke up, and I understand pretending to be in a relationship might not be an attractive option for you, but I don't think you should discount the idea."

Slumping in the chair, Ignacio used the tips of his fingers to rub his temple where a headache had blossomed in the past few minutes. "I need time to think."

"How much time?"

"I don't know!" Ignacio exclaimed in exasperation. "I'll text you my answer once I've had time to figure out what the hell I want to do."

"All right, all right, don't shoot the messenger. I'll hold off Eddie and Delta. Will twenty-four hours be enough time?"

"Yes, that's fine," Ignacio grumbled, though twenty-four years would be preferable.

"I'll give you a call tomorrow."

After the call ended, he sat on the balcony, staring out at the city. Already, his chest felt as if it was caving in. Yesterday, when he had seen Delta, he'd been unprepared and almost suffocated at the sight of her. How the hell was he supposed to manage being in a fake relationship with his ex in front of the world? Paparazzi everywhere. A frenzy of flashing cameras. Their faces splashed across *Page Six* and every grocery store gossip rag. The prying eyes of *TMZ* and *Entertainment Tonight* following their every move.

He thought about the script and proposal in the fireproof box under his bed. He'd sent out multiple copies to potential backers, all without a single bite.

Now, opportunity stared him in the face. All he had to do was... pretend. Pretend that he adored her. Pretend that Delta James, his first and only love, hadn't eviscerated him eleven years ago.

Could this be the only chance he had of getting his film made?

No, there would be another opportunity—one that didn't include becoming entangled with Delta. He'd find a way.

He sent Yvonne the following message: *Not interested.*

Her response came almost immediately.

Delta and her father really want this. They're on their way to you.

Ignacio stared at the text in disbelief.

They had some nerve. Well, they were wasting their time, and he couldn't wait to tell them so.

Chapter Two

In the back of the limousine, Delta James pulled up yet another article on her phone: *Have Actor Ignacio Santana and R&B Artist Delta J Reignited Their Old Flame?*

The writer went on to say, *Could it be true? The playboy of Hollywood and his good girl R&B princess are back together again?*

She skimmed the rest of the article in favor of the photo in the middle, which showed her and Ignacio at the party. They had accidentally bumped into each other, and he reached out to steady her by grabbing her arm. But the photo looked as if he were holding her instead, their eyes locked on each other as she gazed up at him.

No wonder people thought they were back together. Based on the angle, the image was suggestive and had been shared countless times across the Internet, with their names trending on the major social media platforms for hours.

She rubbed her right arm, feeling the phantom burn of his

touch. Eleven years later, and he somehow still managed to affect her profoundly.

"People love a reunion story," her father said, seated beside her.

Edward James was known throughout the music industry as Eddie J, the cutthroat manager who had negotiated the best deals for his singer daughter. Since starting in this business, his mahogany skin had begun to show wrinkles around his eyes, and he'd developed a belly that hinted at his love for alcohol and rich foods, though his mind was as sharp as ever.

"Seems that way," Delta said, gazing out the window.

Except she and Ignacio weren't reuniting. They had barely spoken at all, aside from when he apologized for bumping into her, and she had absolved him of guilt with an "It's okay" and hurried away.

She saw him one other time during the night, across the crowded room, but that was the extent of their interaction. Nonetheless, the two of them together had created shockwaves because of their history. Meeting when they were both thirteen, they became friends first and then much more. They lost their virginity to each other at sixteen, followed by five tumultuous years of breakups and makeups until...

She chewed the inside of her cheek, stopping herself from going down the road of gnawing regret that consumed her to this day.

Delta turned to her father. "Are you sure this is a good idea?"

"Of course I'm sure," he said. "Do you really think I'd take you to meet him if I wasn't confident he'd agree to this? Ignacio has no choice. He needs the publicity as much as you do, and that's the beauty of this whole plan. You'll be helping each other. It's not one-sided. When your 'relationship' is over, you won't owe him, and he won't owe you because you'll both have gotten what you wanted out of the deal."

The deal.

She hated those two words together. More often than not, they caused her problems. "Why couldn't Mom come?"

Her father could be a bit abrupt in his drive for success, while her mother, Jocelyn, often tempered his behavior with her more reasonable approach.

"She's on one of her shopping sprees," he said with a dismissive wave of his hand.

Retail therapy, her mother called her jaunts to spend money. Sometimes she flew out of town to New York or overseas. Delta never complained when a trip ended up going over budget. Shopping was a lot less destructive than the gouging her mother used to do when she was Delta's merchandising manager and let alcohol control her behavior. Removing her mother from that role and giving her the BS title of "advisor" had been a difficult but necessary decision.

"I think we should have given Ignacio more time to consider the idea," Delta said.

"Have I taught you nothing in all these years? Strike while the iron is hot. We couldn't buy this type of publicity if we tried, and delaying would risk having you and Ignacio removed from the spotlight. Even worse, he could find some other way to promote his film and not need you at all. This way, we maintain the urgency of the situation." Her father returned his attention to the open file on his lap.

Delta didn't bother inquiring about what he was looking at. He managed all her affairs and had done so ever since she was a child. The fickle nature of the music industry meant that though she'd had two multi-platinum albums and subsequent successful tours, her third album had not seen the same type of numbers as the first two. Sales had declined, streams dropped off, and she'd had to cancel the latter part of her third tour due to lack of sales.

Bottom line, her father was right. She needed the agreement with Ignacio. Her only concern was getting out of their so-called relationship unscathed.

The chauffeur pulled up to the building where Ignacio lived, and Delta and her father went inside, her heels clicking on the tiled floor. No one bothered them. In fact, they barely glanced in their direction. There was a time she couldn't go out without bodyguards or had to wear disguises. A failing career meant such extremes were no longer an issue.

A man at the front desk called up to Ignacio's apartment, and Delta held her breath as she waited. To her surprise, he granted permission for them to go up.

Inside the elevator, she quickly assessed her appearance. She wore a powder blue jacket and powder blue slacks with clear heels, exposing her toes painted a soft pink color to match her manicure. Under the jacket, she wore a pink bustier and had pulled her hair into a clip-on ponytail. Dark sunglasses covered her eyes, allowing her to hide a little as she steeled her nerves for the meeting with Ignacio.

On the tenth floor, she released a slow breath and walked behind her father to the condo, keeping her eyes on his close-cropped hair, which displayed a sprinkling of gray.

When they stopped at the door, her pulse kicked into higher gear, and her pink nails dug into her palms as she clenched her fists. Despite all that, she was ill-prepared for the stunning man who opened the door before they could knock.

Look up the phrase "movie-star good looks," and there was bound to be a picture of Ignacio Santana in the search results. He stood shirtless in the doorway, wearing only a pair of red boxer briefs. Why was he dressed like that?

She quickly lifted her eyes from the way the material clung

to his thick thighs and showcased his impressive bulge. A lit cigarette hung from the corner of his mouth. He looked like he'd just rolled out of bed, dark stubble on his chin, and his hair tumbled over to one side in an array of brown and honey-blond curls.

His gray eyes met hers behind the sunglasses for a fraction of a second, and the world came to a standstill as she forgot to breathe. He'd always had that effect on her, from the first moment she'd seen him at thirteen. She thought he'd say something to her, but he spoke to her father instead.

"What do you want?" he asked.

Edward straightened his back. At six feet, he was tall but two inches shorter than Ignacio. "We want to talk to you."

Ignacio removed the cigarette from between his lips. "About what?"

Edward sighed. "You know what, but you're not going to make this easy, are you? I'm sure Yvonne told you we were on our way. We want to discuss the viral photo from the other night."

"You came all the way here to talk to me? You couldn't talk over the phone?"

"We were in town and thought it best to have this conversation face-to-face."

Bracing his legs shoulder-width apart, Ignacio folded his arms across his defined chest. "I don't want to talk to you, so you can leave. If you had called, I could have saved you a trip."

"I think you should reconsider. This is a mutually beneficial agreement we're proposing."

"I don't want anything to do with you—or her." His eyes bored into Delta.

His words hit like a hammer to the heart. As she'd feared, this was a bad idea. But she would not allow him to see how his harsh words hurt. She straightened her shoulders and angled her chin higher, staring right back at him.

"Give me five minutes to lay out the idea, and if you're not interested, we'll leave," Edward said.

Ignacio smirked. He knew that was a lie. Her father never gave up that easily. Holding the cigarette between his forefinger and thumb, he took a heavy drag and then blew the smoke in her father's face.

To Edward's credit, he didn't cough or react at all, unlike Delta, who immediately covered her nose to keep the acrid smoke from invading her nostrils.

"You have five minutes." Ignacio turned away from the door and walked deeper into the condo.

Delta gave a delicate cough as she followed both men inside. Goodness, the place was a wreck. Apparently, he'd had one of his famously wild parties the night before. Her gaze landed on a pink and gold stiletto, and something inside her twisted, forcing her to turn away. Ignacio was seldom without female company, and the owner of the shoe was probably buried under the covers of his bed, impatiently waiting for his return.

One of the drawbacks of ending a relationship with a famous man meant, at any time, she could be inundated with images of him enjoying himself with someone—someone who wasn't her.

Ignacio stepped over some trash on the floor, and Delta's eyes zeroed in on the letter "D" tattooed on his right shoulder blade in black ink. She had a tattoo in the same place, but it was an "I." They had gotten the tattoos when they turned eighteen, during one of the periods they had reconciled. The ink was part of a recommitment ceremony they'd held in private.

Now that they were no longer together, it was ridiculous to have the initial of his first name on her body. Whenever she was asked about the letter, she always said the "I" stood for independence. Did he also lie and make up a story about what the "D" stood for? If so, what did he say? That it stood for Danger? Dedication? *Destruction?*

"Party last night?" Edward asked.

Instead of answering, Ignacio sat on the loveseat facing them, crossed his ankle over his knee, and spread his arms wide across the back of the chair. The cigarette rested between two of his fingers.

"I don't suppose you'd consider putting on a shirt and pants?" Edward asked.

"Tick tock. Your time is running out," Ignacio warned, looking like a sexy, swarthy-skinned vagabond with his half-naked body and unkempt hair.

Edward muttered something under his breath. "Here's what I propose. You and Delta pretend you're back together, using all the free publicity generated from your alleged reconciliation. Go on some very public outings, all to keep your name in the press and keep chatter going online about you."

"Why would I join you in misleading the public?"

"Because it's beneficial to you both. The first indie film you directed bombed, and from what I hear, you're having a hard time funding your next passion project."

The muscle above Ignacio's left eye jumped several times. *He's furious.*

"I can raise the money."

Edward shrugged, strolled over to the window and looked at the city before he swiveled to face Ignacio again. "Maybe, eventually, but wouldn't you rather do it sooner rather than later? All we have to do is negotiate the particulars of the 'relationship.' When we want it to end, which red carpet events you'll attend together, talking points. This could be very easy."

"Or very hard."

"We can make it easy. Once we figure out the details, we get the lawyers involved to draw up the contracts."

"If the public finds out we're faking, you realize there could be a huge backlash, potentially destroying our reputations," Ignacio pointed out.

"It's in the best interest of both parties to keep this confidential, and, of course, an ironclad non-disclosure clause will be included in the agreement." Edward made a theatrical pause. "What do you say, Ignacio? Are you in?"

Chapter Three

As silence filled the room, Ignacio continued to smoke, holding the cigarette between his forefinger and middle finger. He turned his attention to Delta, who shifted uncomfortably in the center of the room.

"It's so interesting that years have passed since we've talked, and you bring me this type of... request." He directed the words to her.

"I—"

Edward interrupted his daughter's response. "A request that benefits you both."

Though the older man might be correct, Ignacio had his doubts. He also derived a certain amount of pleasure from making them wait and wonder—would he agree? Would he not?

The publicity could certainly work in his favor, and though he had been staunchly against the ruse when Yvonne initially mentioned the idea, seeing Delta again created a certain...

He didn't know how to define what he was feeling. An

ache. A craving. Something deeper and more urgent than when he had bumped into her at the party and spent the rest of the night tortured by the scent of her perfume on his sleeve.

He smiled slowly, feeling very much like a cat that had swallowed a particularly tasty treat. "I'm in."

He saw the shock in Delta's face by the way her eyebrows lifted toward the ceiling.

"Yes!" Edward clenched his fingers into fists in front of him and shot a look at Delta.

"Under one condition," Ignacio added.

The smile died on Edward's face, and the room became unnaturally silent.

"No contract. This is a handshake deal only."

"No!" Delta removed her sunglasses and turned to her father, silently beseeching him not to go along with the idea.

"Wait a minute, let's hear him out," her father said.

Ignacio pushed to his feet. "A handshake is all I need."

"That's not all I need. It's not binding," Delta said.

The fire in her eyes excited Ignacio and reminded him of their romps between the sheets. The way she would moan and whisper his name, shortening it to *Nacio*. The way she would claw his back, her body soft and trembling against him as he licked every inch of her beautiful dark skin. He shoved away the thoughts before he embarrassed himself by getting an erection in front of the two of them.

"It will be binding to me," he said.

"She's right," Edward said. "We need a written contract with terms so there's no confusion about who does what, when, and how. We need details. Without the details, we'll never know when the contract has been violated."

"Signing an agreement leaves a paper trail, potentially exposing our plans. If I don't do my part in helping with the publicity, do you plan to take me to court and let the world know we've been lying? I don't plan to do that if you fall short."

He practically saw the wheels turning in Edward's head. He knew Ignacio was right but needed reassurances. Ignacio didn't plan to give him any.

"If we don't have a contract—"

"We don't need a contract," Ignacio said firmly. He stubbed out his cigarette on the glass tabletop and blew smoke out the corner of his mouth. "If this is to be believable, all we have to do is behave like a loving couple. I'm an actor. It won't be a problem for me."

And the performance would be his greatest to date.

"We should be available for red carpet appearances and other major events. We should post each other on our social media accounts. The usual things that couples do," he added.

"How do we know you'll hold up your end of the bargain?" Edward asked.

"You don't." Ignacio shifted his gaze to Delta and said the next words directly to her. "You'll have to trust me."

By the grimace of discomfort on her face, she knew exactly what he was referring to.

"We need to talk for a moment." Edward placed a hand on his daughter's arm and guided her out of earshot to the front door.

Ignacio waited while they had an animated conversation. She was clearly against the idea, but daddy dearest would convince her to go along with the plan. He always did.

Edward controlled her life, and she fell in line. No matter how questionable the terms of the "agreement," Ignacio understood the most important thing to that man—to them—was the potential windfall. Her career would be back on top, and it was worth the risk of joining with him—without a contract—to get her there.

The conversation ended, and they returned to face Ignacio.

"We've come to a decision," Edward began. "We agree to your terms. This arrangement will last as long as it takes for you to secure funding for your film and for her to release her first single."

"How long before she releases her first single?" Ignacio asked.

"She's been in the recording studio. Her first single should be out in a few months. Does that work for you?"

"Fine by me. As long as she performs her girlfriend duties to the best of her ability," Ignacio drawled.

"Of course she will," Edward said, sounding offended. "And so will you?"

"Yes, but Delta hasn't said much since the two of you arrived. I want to hear her say she's in agreement and will perform her girlfriend duties to the best of her ability."

Edward nudged her, and she glared at Ignacio. If she could rip his head off with those pretty pink nails, he was certain she would.

"I agree to perform my girlfriend duties in this ridiculous arrangement to the best of my ability," she said, barely getting the words past stiff lips.

Ignacio stepped closer, completely ignoring her father. "Can I trust you, Delta?"

"Yes."

"I hope so. That hasn't always been the case."

She angled her head higher. "There's a lot at stake for both of us. I don't think it would be in anyone's best interest to reveal the truth about our arrangement or to renege." She smiled tightly, with no teeth, which wasn't a smile at all.

"Are the two of you done?" Edward's deep voice interrupted. "You should probably brush aside your hangups for the overall good."

His response suggested that he had forgotten his role in their split eleven years ago. Delta had broken his heart, crushed his spirit, and almost caused him to give up on his love of making movies. And she had used her father as her messenger of destruction.

Ignacio slid his gaze to Edward. "I'd like to speak to Delta in private, please."

Her father looked surprised, then straightened his shoulders. "All right. I'll step outside and let you talk." With a final glance at his daughter, he went onto the balcony and closed the door behind him.

Standing in the room alone with his ex, Ignacio experienced the unexpected crack of electricity. Delta was born to be a star. A dancer and singer with lethal curves, she was beautiful and sexy, with dark chestnut skin, dark eyes, and thick lashes naturally curling back toward her lids. Her pouty lips invited kisses, whether bare or covered in maroon lipstick like they were today.

"I don't start filming my next movie for six months, so I'm moving back to Atlanta during that period. It'll give me time to polish my script and work on securing funding. I had planned to rent a place, but if you and I are going to pretend to be a couple, you should come house-hunting with me. Nothing says we're a couple like looking for a place together."

"Fine by me," she said in a bored tone.

Her lack of enthusiasm aggravated him. "If you don't want to do this, say the word and I'll walk away."

Her pretty eyes narrowed. "Your flippant attitude isn't fooling me, Ignacio. If my father's right, and you're having difficulty securing funding for your movie, you're in the same situation I am. So as much as you'd like to pretend you're doing me a favor, you need me as much as I need you."

Need her? He'd spent the last eleven years *not* needing her, and he sure as hell wasn't about to start now.

Ignacio stepped closer, looking down at her with insolence. "That's where you're wrong, Delta, *mi amor*. I don't need you. Don't *ever* make the mistake of thinking that I need you."

The tension in the room quadrupled, and he felt the change in the stiffness of his muscles. Turning away, he walked to the love seat to give himself time to calm down.

"You couldn't wait to say that, could you?"

"I wanted to make sure we understood each other."

She swallowed, then her expression shuttered as she hid her true feelings. She'd always been good at masking her emotions. After all, she'd convinced him that she loved him, right up until she had her father do her dirty work and dump him like trash.

"Believe me, we do."

"*Bueno.*" Ignacio rested his hands on his hips and caught the fleeting movement of her eyes on his chest. His nipples tightened under the heat of her gaze, and he gained a certain satisfaction from knowing that maybe she wasn't completely immune to him. "We need to discuss the issue of... sex."

Delta's eyes widened in alarm. "It's a fake relationship," she said pointedly.

He smirked. "I know. I wasn't suggesting we have sex, unless...?" He arched an eyebrow.

Her lips flattened into a grim line—as much as her full, luscious lips could.

"What were you suggesting?" she asked.

"I wanted to remind you that during this period neither of us can have sex with other people."

"Abstinence is not a problem for me, but you, on the other hand..." She smiled tartly.

"I can abstain."

"Can you?" She looked around his wrecked apartment, her gaze landing on the stiletto in the corner.

"Don't worry about me. I've been known to go without sex for months. I've had a lot of practice," he said.

During their tumultuous five years as a couple, during their off periods, he had remained faithful to her and kept away from other women. Foolish, in retrospect. He should have been living it up instead of being loyal to a woman who deemed her career significantly more important than their relationship. A woman who strung him along until the very last moment.

"We're on the same page," Delta said in a cool tone.

"In that case, we need to keep the rumor mill going about us. I think we should make a big splash."

"An unofficial but official announcement?" she suggested.

"Exactly."

The room fell silent as they thought.

"What about the Black and Gold Music Experience?" Delta proposed. "It takes place next week, and I attend every year. We could make our debut as a couple on the red carpet."

Ignacio nodded slowly. He'd gone before but hadn't attended in recent years. "That would be perfect." He paused as another, crazier idea came to mind. "You seem very committed to making this work."

"Of course I'm committed."

"How committed are you? Are you willing to do anything?"

Her eyes narrowed a fraction. "Within reason," she said carefully.

"You're sure you're up to this?"

In some ways, the question was directed at himself. Physical attraction aside, Delta had proven years ago that she had no attachment to him, and no doubt she felt even less now. He, however—how would he handle being in close proximity to the woman he had intended to marry? Especially since his body still wanted her, and her presence caused a strange tightening in his chest.

"I'm ready," Delta replied with vehemence.

"Good," Ignacio said with deep satisfaction. "Here's my idea. I think we should move in together."

Chapter Four

Delta's eyes widened. "*Excuse me?* Um, no."

Ignacio bristled at her response and became more determined to make it happen. "And why not?"

"We can behave convincingly by meeting up every now and again. The Black and Gold event, going to restaurants, the usual sightings. Moving in together is too disruptive."

"I disagree. Living together makes perfect sense and will show everyone that we're serious this time, making our reconciliation more believable."

"I don't agree." Delta pressed a hand to her temple as if she had a headache. "I have a house in Atlanta."

"And your family lives with you. When I'm in Atlanta, I often stay at my mother's. Renting a place and moving in together gives us the opportunity to present to the world that *we're* each other's family now."

"Why is that necessary? I'm not convinced."

"Then how about this? Moving in together will help me."

"And I should care because...?"

He clenched his jaw but bit back the angry words that almost spilled from his lips. "Right now, the media portrays me as a wild partying playboy."

"Gee, I wonder why." She smiled sweetly.

She really knew how to push his buttons.

Ignacio continued. "If they see we're living together, they'll write different types of stories about me, which could send a positive message to potential investors."

"I hear you, but there's a problem you haven't considered."

"Which is?"

As far as Ignacio was concerned, he'd considered every angle. For years, he leaned into the media's characterization, hosting wild parties and rotating women in and out of his life with ease. It wasn't all bad. It kept women from thinking they had a shot at tying him down and making him monogamous, of becoming the first Mrs. Ignacio Santana.

But now he wondered if his behavior had lowered expectations regarding his business acumen. Did backers wonder if he could be trusted? Pretending to be monogamous with Delta could help his image, thereby increasing his chance of finding an investor.

"You've forgotten about household staff," Delta answered. "They're going to notice we're not sleeping in the same bed."

"We'll have them sign NDAs, as usual."

"There's still a chance of a leak. Do you really want to take that risk?"

Ignacio scraped his fingers through his hair in frustration and paced away from her. She was right. They couldn't risk chatter from staff. He had a loyal housekeeper who would be temporarily moving from LA to live with him in Atlanta, but there were other people, like the cleaners, who would be local hires. Could they be trusted to keep their mouths shut, or would they break when someone came along and offered a nice sum of money in exchange for knowledge?

He swung to face Delta, who was standing in the middle of the room with her arms crossed over her midsection. "Then we sleep in the same bed."

If he thought her eyes had gone wide before, they practically bulged out of their sockets at that suggestion. Then she burst into laughter.

"I'm glad you think this is funny."

"You're serious?" she asked in an incredulous voice.

"Yes, and the more I think about it, the better I like the idea."

"That's a terrible idea."

"I disagree."

"Think about what you're saying."

"It's for appearance's sake, Delta. As you pointed out, we can't risk having someone on staff disclose we're sleeping separately. That doesn't exactly confirm we're a loving couple back together again. And what's the problem with sleeping in the same bed? Neither of us has to answer to anyone, so there's no one to be concerned that we'll..."

"We'll what?"

"Have sex."

Her lips parted in silent shock.

"Unless...?" he drawled.

"Never," she said firmly.

"Never say never. We used to rock the bed, remember?"

"Did we? I barely remember. It was eleven years ago, and I was much younger."

"Does that mean you've gotten better or worse at sex?"

"None of your damn business," she snapped.

"Want to know about me?" Ignacio asked, dropping his voice to a silken timbre.

"No."

A smirk touched his lips. "I've gotten better."

Her breath unmistakably hitched, and catching her reaction was intensely rewarding and... arousing.

She quickly assessed Ignacio from his chest to his feet before bringing her gaze higher again. "Is this what I have to look forward to? Your harassment?"

"I'm letting you know the options available."

"I don't need to know the options, thanks. I'll be practicing abstinence for the next six months."

"You don't have to." He needed to stop pushing so hard, but he couldn't help himself.

She took a frustrated breath and let it out. "We'll sleep in the same room but not the same bed. I'll sleep on the floor or in a chair or something."

"For six months?"

"What other choice is there?" she demanded.

"We can share the bed. I promise I won't maul you."

She shot a skeptical look in his direction.

"We need to make a decision, Delta."

"Fine. We'll sleep in the same bed with pillows between us."

She looked so uncomfortable, he couldn't help laughing, which pissed her off more and caused her to send a glare in his direction.

"Now we need to run the idea by your father and see what he thinks."

"Let's not tell him we're sharing a bed, okay?"

"Are you sure? I'd be interested to hear what he has to say about the arrangement."

"I would not."

Smirking, Ignacio signaled through the glass at her father.

Edward re-entered the living room and looked from one to the other. "Any new developments I should know about?"

Ignacio sat on the loveseat. "We discussed attending the Black and Gold Music Experience to make our relationship official. We're also going house-hunting. I'll make sure my people tip off the media so we can get some candid shots published. What do you think about the two of us moving in together?"

Edward slowly nodded. "I think it's an excellent idea."

The look Delta sent in her father's direction was... interesting, and not in a good way. He had to admit, he was a little surprised how easily Edward had gone along with the idea, and Delta must have been too. He saw disappointment in her expression, and something inside him twisted, making him feel protective of her. Not that she wanted his protection.

"So you don't have any reservations about us living together for six whole months?" Ignacio asked.

"None whatsoever," Edward replied. "If the two of you move in together, it lends credence to the idea that you're a couple again. I say go for it."

"I'll let the two of you finalize any additional details. I'll be in the car." Delta stalked out and closed the door none too gently.

Edward watched her leave and then shook his head. "I don't know what gets into her sometimes. This is an opportunity to revive her career with just a little bit of sacrifice."

"Thank goodness she has you in her corner."

"Exactly."

He had no idea Ignacio was being sarcastic.

"We'll be in touch." Edward stopped on his way out. "One more thing. I want to make sure you don't have any long-term plans for my daughter. She's focused on selling records and doesn't need any distractions."

Fury billowed inside Ignacio as he recalled that day eleven years ago when Edward showed up at the airport to let him know Delta would not be meeting him. That their relationship was truly over and done with, and she was going to focus on her singing career.

"Don't worry, I haven't forgotten her career is the priority."

"Good. That way we can all get what we want. You included."

Edward left then, leaving Ignacio to ruminate on the past. He would do well to remember his previous interactions with the James family, and how at twenty-one, he had been left desolate and broken after Delta decided at the last minute that she would not elope with him.

He snatched a tumbler from a side table and hurled it across the room. It hit the wall and shattered into little pieces.

Chapter Five

Delta slammed the car door and marched ahead of her father into her L.A. home, one of several she had purchased over the years. She also slammed the front door and stomped up the stairs.

"Delta!" Her father's voice cracked at her from the doorway.

She stopped, closed her eyes, and counted backwards from ten to calm down. Slowly, she faced him, fixing a blank expression on her face, which she had learned to do a long time ago to keep people from knowing her true thoughts. "Yes?"

"You didn't say a word to me the entire ride back."

She wanted to point out he hadn't said a word to her either, but instead asked, "What is there to say?"

He shut the door much more softly than she had and walked over to the staircase. "There's no need to be disrespectful."

Normally, she held her tongue and acquiesced to his decision-making because she believed he had her best interests at heart, but this time she was certain he'd made a horrible mistake and couldn't stay quiet.

"It's bad enough you agreed we could work with Ignacio without a contract, which goes against everything you've ever taught me about business, by the way. You used to be a lawyer, for goodness' sake! But then you agreed we should move in together without a second thought. It's a terrible idea! You know it. I know it."

"Not all deals have to be written down, and he had a valid point about the potential for a leak if we signed a contract. Everything will be fine. You'll see."

"Sure," Delta said with a tight smile.

"Get your head in the game. This is your chance to get back on top of the charts and prove to the record label and the naysayers that you still have what it takes to be a star. The point of this entire ruse is to use the publicity generated by your relationship with Ignacio to your advantage. All you have to do is get in the recording studio and knock it out of the park."

He made the next steps sound so simple, and under normal circumstances, she appreciated his pep talks, but no amount of rah-rah-rah would work this time. They were going to be working with her ex, and the young man she'd fallen in love with was long gone. The thirty-two-year-old man in his place hated her. His contempt was palpable.

"Right. I'll do that. Knock it out of the park," Delta said with feigned enthusiasm.

She didn't wait for her father's reply. She marched the rest of the way up the stairs and down the hall to the master suite and shoved her way through the double doors. Flinging herself across the king-size bed, she buried her face in the thick comforter.

Her chest hurt. Her head hurt. Everything hurt. There had not been a smidgen of warmth in Ignacio's expression the entire time they talked. How could they possibly move in together and pretend to be in love?

Maybe he could do it. He was an actor, after all, but for her, the performance would be a struggle. And not because she wasn't attracted to him. She was still *very* much attracted to him.

She used to love his teasing kisses and playing in his luxurious brown curls. It pained her to watch his films where he showered affection on his on-screen love interests. The love scenes were especially difficult to watch. Two years ago, all she heard was how great the chemistry was between him and his leading lady in the film *Sleeping Poets*. He had played the role of a literature professor under suspicion for murder, having an affair with the female detective investigating the case. He'd looked so delicious in those glasses and tweed jackets that she couldn't blame the poor detective for falling for his charms.

But the love scenes...

Delta shivered now, her nipples tightening against the mattress. His husky groans and the way he gripped the actress's thighs as he rocked between her legs had looked too real. Too sensual. Too familiar.

Living with him twenty-four hours a day for months would be torture. How the heck was she supposed to pretend to feel nothing while her body burned for him?

At a soft knock on the door, Delta sat up. "Come in."

Her younger sister, Vivian, rolled in on her wheelchair and closed the door behind her. She was three years younger and Delta's best friend.

The sisters had been named after their father's older sisters who had died in an accident when he was a teenager. Both women had been singers, and that night they were on their way home from a gig at a local club when their vehicle was T-boned by a drunk driver. Though he had never said it, Delta believed her father pushed her so hard as a way to achieve the career his sisters had never reached because of their premature deaths.

"Somebody had a bad day," Vivian observed, shoving her gold-framed glasses higher on her nose.

"That's definitely me." Delta removed her heels and tossed them across the room.

Vivian followed the motion and lifted an eyebrow. "What's going on with you?"

"We went to see Ignacio today."

Her sister looked surprised. "How did the meeting go?"

Delta blew out a breath of frustration and hopped off the bed. Resting her hands on her hips, she paced the carpeted floor of her bedroom. "He hates me."

"He doesn't hate you."

"He literally hates me, Viv."

"Well, what are you going to do? You need each other, right? That's what Dad said."

"Ignacio says he doesn't need me."

"He can't still be angry about what happened. It's been what... ten, eleven years?"

"Eleven." Delta stopped pacing and faced her sister across the room. "I hurt him."

"You were hurting too. It wasn't easy for you not to go to him."

"He doesn't know that. He thinks I didn't care." She blew out another breath. "I can't blame him because that's how I acted. We were supposed to run away together, and I... I blew it."

Her sister's expression turned sympathetic. "You were young and at the beginning of your career. He asked you to marry him. That's a big step."

Delta's shoulders slumped. "I should have gone to him when he asked me to."

"Why didn't you?"

Delta turned away and wrapped her arms around herself. "I don't know."

But that wasn't true. She did know why.

At the age of nine, Vivian was diagnosed with a spinal cord tumor after experiencing back pain and trouble walking. The diagnosis was devastating. Doctors were able to remove the tumor, but the surgery caused nerve damage, leaving Vivian paralyzed from the waist down.

Over the years, she had undergone multiple surgeries to correct spinal curvature and muscle atrophy. Her poor sister had been poked and prodded by specialists all over the world, subjected to nerve stimulation procedures and orthopedic treatments. Though Delta hoped for a miracle, her sister had accepted her condition, though not in a fatalistic way. She regularly went to physical therapy and used a high-tech wheelchair to get around.

Delta never left to be with Ignacio because her parents had sat her down and told her the hard truth: they couldn't afford her sister's surgeries without her. Even if they both went back to work, her sister's medical bills and care would cripple them financially. So she made the tough decision to walk away from her relationship with the man she loved and focus on building her career—a career that eventually paid her millions of dollars and allowed her to support her sister and the rest of her family.

"You can't keep living in the past, D," Vivian said.

"I know, but this is going to be difficult." She turned away from the window and faced her sister. "You know what? I can handle it."

"Of course you can, but people are going to try to find out why the two of you broke up in the first place. Do you plan to tell the truth?"

"First of all, I'm sure he wouldn't want the world to know

he got dumped, and do you think *I* want to get tarred and feathered for being the dummy who broke up with *Ignacio Santana, the Latin heartthrob?*"

Vivian giggled at the exaggerated Spanish accent she used.

Delta grinned at her sister's reaction, but then she let the smile fade from her face. "Ignacio starts filming his next movie in six months. That's how long we have to sell our relationship and accomplish our individual goals."

Vivian studied her in silence.

Delta tilted her head to the side. "What?"

"How was it seeing him again and talking to him?"

Delta shrugged. "No big deal."

"I mean..." Vivian seemed to be choosing her words carefully. "Do you have any feelings left for him? It's been a long time, but I wondered..."

"Whatever feelings I had are long gone."

"Honestly?"

"Of course. Do you really think I'd still be hung up on my first boyfriend?"

"You two were so in love. I was going through surgeries and didn't get to see you together much, but I remember how you talked about him, and I remember seeing photos of the two of you. Everyone thought you made a cute couple."

Delta swallowed past the ache in her throat. As close as they were, she couldn't admit the truth to her sister. That she had gone so far as to write love songs about him. In one in particular—"I Don't Miss You"—she had poured out her heart and released all the turmoil and pain inside. She would never let anyone see that song. The lyrics were too raw. Too personal.

"We broke up a long time ago. In the meantime, we've both been involved with other people, and he was engaged to that actress not long after we split." Miraculously, she kept the bitterness out of her voice.

"Everyone knew the relationship was a rebound thing. They didn't last."

"Doesn't matter. He moved on, I moved on, and we're both in our thirties—older and wiser."

"Definitely older," Vivian said carefully.

Delta narrowed her eyes at her sister and placed her hands on her hips. "Are you saying I'm not wiser?"

Vivian laughed. "No! But I'll believe the two of you are done when at the end of the six months you go your separate ways and move on with your lives."

"Well, I'm here to tell you that's exactly what will happen," Delta said.

"Okay, cool. So what's the first item on the agenda?"

"We agreed to attend the Black and Gold Music Experience for our first official outing as a couple. Then we're going to become more visible around Atlanta, including going house-hunting."

"You're moving in together?" Vivian asked in surprise.

"Unfortunately."

"Interesting..."

"It would be, if we were in a real relationship. I hope this whole thing doesn't backfire." She paused. "In the meantime, I have to work on my album, but I don't feel very inspired by the songs, and it's obvious in my performance."

"I'm not worried. You always pull through."

Delta smiled appreciatively. Her sister was her biggest cheerleader and always had her back. "Thanks, Viv. What would I do without you?"

"Lose your mind. Fall apart."

"Somebody's a little full of herself." Delta tossed a tufted pillow from the bed at her sister.

Laughing, Vivian tossed it back. "I can't believe you would bully a disabled person."

Delta gasped in mock outrage. "Oh, please! You're always telling me what to do and when to do it. You're the biggest bully I know."

Vivian smirked. "And don't you forget it. Just because I'm in a wheelchair doesn't mean I can't take you down."

Delta crossed her arms. "I'd like to see you try."

Vivian gave her a wicked grin. "I will run over your toes without a second thought."

Delta let out a laugh and held up her hands in surrender. "Fine. You win. Truce. Sheesh."

Vivian gave a regal nod. "That's what I thought." She headed toward the door and paused. "I'm going to pack for our flight to Atlanta tomorrow, but if you need anything, you'll let me know, right?"

Sometimes Delta believed Vivian genuinely forgot she was the younger sibling and Delta should be taking care of *her*. Not that she minded. The music industry was a cutthroat business, and it was nice to know someone was in her corner—someone with no ulterior motives.

"You're the only sane person in this family. Of course I will," Delta said.

Laughing, Vivian left, closing the door behind her.

The smile dropped off Delta's face. She prayed this album was a success. That was the only outcome that made participating in this fiasco worth her while—and worth facing Ignacio and his wrath.

Chapter Six

Normally, Delta's dressing room was a place of serenity and calm, but tonight it was chaotic.

Her entire glam squad was in attendance to get her ready for the Black and Gold Music Experience. Two members of her team were men—her makeup artist and Pierre, her personal shopper and fashion consultant. Both had flown in from LA. The two women were her hairstylist and nail technician, both based out of Atlanta.

Her publicist, Rochelle, sat in the corner, her raven hair hanging in bone-straight sheets that hid half her face as she texted. At the event, she would accompany Delta as she strolled the red carpet.

Dressed in a white robe, Delta sat in front of her vanity chatting with fans on Instagram Live as she prepared for the big night.

She let out a peal of laughter at a comment from one of the viewers. "It's a lot of work to look the way we do. I wish I woke up like this," she said.

She extended her right hand so the nail technician could

work on her nails while the stylist gently pulled her hair out of huge rollers.

Leaning slightly forward, Delta read the next question on the iPad screen. "Are you going alone or is Ignacio Santana going to escort you?"

Instead of answering, she smiled coyly and purposely fueled speculation by saying, "I'm looking forward to an amazing evening. The Music Experience is one of my favorite events to attend each year."

Emoji-filled comments raced up the screen—exactly the reaction she had anticipated. She felt a surge of guilt at the excited comments but reminded herself that what she and Ignacio were doing was a necessary evil. There was no other way to get what they both wanted.

Minutes later, she turned off the live stream and let the team finish their work. Almost an hour later, she examined her appearance in the floor-length mirror.

Standing off to the side, Rochelle eyed her from head to toe. "You look stunning," she gushed.

Delta took the compliment in stride, smiling her *Thank you.* Her team had truly done an amazing job. First, her hair was styled in loose curls that tumbled onto her shoulders. Her hair didn't always behave, but it was being good tonight.

Her shimmering gown was a Balmain original. The lavender color complemented her dark skin and hugged her curves, the high slit on the left revealing her toned leg, a testament to her hard work with a personal trainer. Her makeup artist had dusted glittering bronzer onto her shoulders, which were shown off by the strapless design of the dress.

Pierre's dark brown hair fell over his forehead as he lowered to his haunches and completed her outfit by slipping a pair of Piferi metallic gold sandals with ankle straps on her feet. "Now for the finishing touch," he said, fastening a diamond choker around her neck.

Delta tossed her hair and squared her shoulders the way she had been taught in etiquette classes as a young girl. "How do I look?"

"Stunning," the nail technician whispered.

Hands on her hips, Delta did a slow turn, taking her time to complete another thorough examination of her appearance in the mirror. As much as she enjoyed the comfort of sweatpants and jeans, at heart, she was a girly girl who loved dressing up for industry parties and red carpet events.

Her team applauded.

"You're going to be the talk of the red carpet—in more ways than one," Rochelle said with a wink.

Part of the agreement between her and Ignacio had been to tell as few people as possible about their fake relationship so the truth wouldn't leak. Her publicist knew, and so did her inner circle—her parents and her sister. He had agreed that only his manager and personal assistant would be told.

"So the two of you are really back together?" The question came from her hairstylist.

"We are," Delta said, infusing her voice with enthusiasm—the way a woman in love would.

Lying was never easy, and it was especially difficult to do to people who cared about you, but she forced a smile to her lips.

"Oh, I'm happy for you!" The nail technician gave her a quick hug.

"Thank you."

What a nightmare it was going to be when they "broke up."

Rochelle checked her phone. "Okay, everybody, we gotta go. The limo is pulling up. Pierre, you're riding with me. Let's go, people!"

There was a flurry of activity as they all grabbed their

belongings. Delta picked up a bluish-gray stone from her dresser and dropped it into her purse. Her good luck charm. Then she hustled out of the dressing room with everyone else and crossed the floor of the bedroom suite into the hallway. Vivian's door cracked open as they passed her room.

Delta immediately stopped and spread her arms wide, showing off for her sister.

Vivian gave the expected bright smile. "You look gorgeous!"

"Thank you!" Delta blew her a kiss and caught up with her team.

Holding Pierre's arm, she carefully walked down the stairs and out the front door as a white limousine pulled into the circular driveway.

As soon as Delta saw the vehicle, every muscle in her body tightened. Ava, her bodyguard, hopped out of the front passenger seat wearing a dark pantsuit the same color as her buzz-cut hair.

Then Ignacio emerged from the back of the limo. Delta's chest tightened and, annoyingly, her heart tripped over itself. She hated her reaction to him. It was innate, automatic, instinctual. She had zero control, which angered as well as disgusted her.

He moved with the smooth, relaxed gait of a man accustomed to commanding the attention of those around him. He wore his hair down around his face, his appearance scrumptious in a charcoal Tom Ford suit that draped perfectly over his body. His crisp white shirt was undone at the collar, lending an air of casual sophistication to his appearance.

When he stopped in front of her, she straightened her back.

"You..." he paused, as if trying to find the right words.

Something in his eyes flashed—a vaguely familiar expression she had seen in the past. An expression that was usually the prelude to passion-filled whispers and a fiery toss beneath the sheets as their bodies strained against each other. His hand at her throat. His lips on her neck. But he schooled his features into an impassive expression, causing her to think she must have imagined what she saw.

"You look amazing."

If she didn't know better, she'd believe he meant the words by the way his eyes scanned her body, coming to rest on her exposed left thigh before making their way back to her face.

But the sentence had been spoken without emotion, in a perfunctory manner—as if he felt obligated to say it instead of there being any sincerity behind the compliment.

"Thanks," Delta said tightly, if for no other reason than for appearance's sake.

Ignacio slipped his hand to the small of her back, the heat from his touch penetrating the material of her dress and raising the temperature in her blood.

He lowered his lips to her ear as if he were whispering a naughty secret. "Remember to smile. We're supposed to be madly in love and experiencing the excitement of our newfound relationship."

She fought the shiver that undulated through her body as his warm, minty breath brushed her sensitive skin.

He wanted fake. She could be fake.

Delta shot a flirtatious, sidelong glance at him. "Thank you for the reminder, baby. How could I forget?" She spoke sweetly in a whisper, punctuating her words with a smile and touching his clean-shaven cheek with the tips of her fingers.

His jaw firmed and his gray eyes darkened momentarily before he said in a curt voice, "We should go."

He nudged her forward with his hand at her spine, and they made their way to the limousine, where the driver now waited beside the open door.

"I'll meet you there!" Rochelle called. Her car was parked up front. She and Pierre hopped in and took off.

Delta slid onto the leather seat, and Ignacio sat beside her. When the door shut, unexpected panic erupted inside her, and her heart started racing.

This was it. They were about to perform for all the people at the event and those watching at home, and they had to convince every last one of them that they were together again and happy.

"What's so funny?" Ignacio asked.

She must have laughed out loud by accident but decided to be honest. "I think this whole charade is ridiculous. Crazy." She kept her voice low, watching as the driver slid behind the wheel and Ava reclaimed her place at the front.

Resting a hand atop his knee, Ignacio relaxed against the leather seat. "You could always back out."

Delta tossed him a scathing look. "You first."

After a brief pause, Ignacio rolled up the partition so they could have privacy. "Let's remember what's at stake, shall we? We both have something to gain if we play our roles correctly."

"Play our roles. Easy for you to say. You're an actor."

He made walking the red carpet look easy. Maybe because his parents had been in the entertainment business for years, and he'd been in the public eye since he was a child.

"What you do is acting too. You play a role as a singer and performer. I've seen your dance routines with your partners on stage. Shouldn't be too hard to pretend you have feelings for me."

"But I actually like them," Delta said.

Adjusting his cuff, Ignacio laughed. The sound was dry and without humor. "Just do what I do when I'm with you. Fake it."

Delta shot him her best kiss-my-ass smile. "I'll do my best."

Then she focused her attention on the outside scenery. She had no intention of talking to him for the rest of the trip.

Chapter Seven

She smelled like jasmine. Delicious. Sweet. Tempting.

Ignacio gazed out the window at the cars and buildings whizzing by on the highway, restlessly tapping his knee, his thoughts never far from the woman sitting nearby, testing his patience and making his groin ache.

Under different circumstances with anyone else, the limo provided plenty of space, but with Delta riding with him, it was simply too small. Her scent wrapped around him like a soft, invisible fabric, urging him to move closer. He breathed her in, and longing pressed hard into his chest—a warning that he was already in too deep. How ridiculous that her scent could make his pulse race and his thoughts scatter. But that was the magic of Delta James. She was effortlessly intoxicating, whether or not she meant to be.

He'd known spending time together would be a bad idea, but he'd had no idea how bad. His attraction to her was fucking annoying. The minute he saw her standing in front of her home, his tongue might as well have rolled out between his teeth like a cartoon character. She was exquisite in the lavender gown, and her hair looked sensational. He instantly wanted to mess up her perfect hairstyle with back shots as he gripped the strands from behind. What man wouldn't?

The ultimate had been when she shot him that little flirty glance from beneath her curled lashes. She had to have known what she was doing. For several seconds, he ceased to think. His entire body went hot, as if gasoline had been poured into his veins and then ignited with a match. Before this was all over, Delta James was going to be the death of him. Of that, he was certain.

To his relief, the limousine finally arrived near the Astoria Grand Hotel and rolled to a stop. The ten-story landmark had been built in the 1920s and dripped with charm and history. The Black and Gold Music Experience took place there every fall, honoring excellence in music and recognizing artists for their impact on society. The annual event celebrated their achievements, from electrifying live performances to unforgettable contributions to film soundtracks, showcasing how music inspires, connects, and enriches lives.

Ava climbed out of the limousine first and surveyed the area like a hawk. At the same time, Ignacio's bodyguard, Randall—who had arrived ahead of them—positioned himself at the back end of the car. Well over six feet tall, he wore a dark suit and scanned the crowd with practiced vigilance.

Though Ignacio loved his career as an actor, this was the aspect of being a celebrity that he disliked the most. Unfortunately, some fans could become obsessive. He once had a stalker break into his home and climb into his bed to wait for him. While he felt sorry for the woman, the entire ordeal had been nerve-racking.

What happened was a thankfully rare occurrence, but he needed multiple close protection officers most days. On a night like tonight, he only required Randall since the venue had its own security.

Randall sent a subtle nod to the chauffeur, and he climbed out of the car.

"This is it," Ignacio said to Delta. "Show time."

For a split second, their gazes met in the car's dim interior, and he saw a flicker of nervousness cross her features. He felt it too. The nervous energy. The anticipation of entering the unknown and putting on the performance of a lifetime.

The driver opened the door, and a rush of noise spilled into the car, breaking the cocoon of quiet inside. Camera shutters clicked in rapid succession, reporters called out questions to the invitees as they arrived, and the high-pitched squeals of excited fans packed behind barricades could be heard.

Ignacio emerged from the vehicle and adjusted the cuffs of his jacket. He was in his element, engaging the cheering crowd with a short wave before turning to help Delta.

"Ready?"

"Always," she replied.

She took his hand, and he clenched his jaw against the crackle of electricity that danced across his skin. The moment Delta stepped out, the crowd went berserk.

"Ohmigod, it's Delta J!" a young woman shrieked from the fan section, followed by a chorus of voices shouting for the couple.

There was no going back now. They had to stay the course and hope they'd get what they wanted. The roles they had taken on would be played out for the world to see, splashed across magazine covers and commented on by fans, detractors, and media.

Holding hands, they walked toward the edge of the carpet. Two members of Delta's team—her publicist, Rochelle, and a slender man—approached immediately. They adjusted Delta's gown and diamond choker and dabbed powder on her nose, though Ignacio hadn't noticed anything wrong with her appearance. She looked as sensational as when they had picked her up.

They continued onto the carpet, this time with Delta's hand in the crook of his elbow. He could feel her fingers pressing lightly into the fine fabric of his jacket.

The cheers from the fans were deafening as they screamed their names and begged for autographs. They paused to sign a few, with Ignacio reaching over one woman's head to take a black-and-white photo of himself and sign it. He handed it back to the owner, who jumped up and down as if she had inherited a fortune.

"I can't believe you're really back together," said a young woman directly in front of him, practically vibrating with tears of excitement.

Ignacio shot a faint smile at Delta. "Some things are meant to be." Damn, he was good. He deserved an award for Best Actor. Delta's answering smile was just as convincing.

Rochelle came over and gently guided them toward the waiting media. The camera flashes intensified. Ahead, Ignacio spotted Victor Creed, a platinum-selling pop/R&B artist. He and Delta had done a duet on his last album. He greeted them with a brief nod and then posed.

Finally, Ignacio and Delta arrived at the main backdrop, where the press congregated for the money shots. A steady stream of yelling ensued.

"Delta! Ignacio! Over here!"

"Delta, can we see that gorgeous smile?"

"Show us the dress, Delta!"

"Ignacio! Ignacio!"

They struck their poses, and then Ignacio stepped aside so Delta could have the limelight for a moment. She did an over-the-shoulder move, one that he'd seen her execute numerous times before. His attention narrowed to the "I" tattooed on her back—his initial, and at the time she got it, her commitment to him. Had it really all been a lie? A sick game she had been playing?

He studied her profile as if the answer would appear before him, but all he saw was beauty, style, and grace. The camera loved her. She continued showing off the back of the dress, which had a jeweled design that ran straight down the middle of her back and over the curve of her plump behind.

Memories from the past flooded him—torturous thoughts of his tongue dragging up the crack of her ass, of gripping her hips and thrusting into her from behind while she gripped the pillows and cried out his name. *Nacio.*

Ignacio wiped away a bead of sweat that had formed on his forehead.

Moments later, he stepped closer and pulled Delta against his side, one hand resting low on her back, her arm curled around his waist. Her soft breast pressed into his side, and his nose filled with the scent of her perfume. Finally, Rochelle ushered them farther down the line, and Ignacio breathed easier, creating space between them. He hadn't realized how much being in such close proximity to Delta had caused him to tense up.

As they strolled into the dimly lit venue, a female voice cut through the quieter hum of voices and activity. "Ignacio! Delta! Over here!"

Brenda Morrison Santorini, the East Coast editor of *The Entertainment Report*, based out of Los Angeles, waved them over.

Ignacio guided Delta to Brenda.

"Brenda, what are you doing here?" he asked, giving her air kisses.

"Trying to get the scoop on the two of you," she replied.

Her skin was amaretto-brown. She had full lips and a tapered cut that flattered her oval face.

"Don't you have people to do this for you?"

"I do, but two of my top people are out with the flu, so here I am, doing the grunt work," she said with a smile. "Delta, you look fabulous, as always."

"Thank you, Brenda." More air kisses.

Brenda wasted no time in asking the tough question. "How does it feel to be back together after all these years?" She stuck a mic in Delta's face.

Delta let out a soft laugh. To her credit, it sounded completely natural. "Like coming home."

Brenda's eyebrows lifted slightly, but he could see she was eating it up. "What led to the reunion?"

Keeping an arm around Delta's waist, Ignacio answered this time. "Timing is everything. Sometimes relationships don't work out, and later, when we gain clarity, we realize what's missing and can course-correct."

"Will it last this time?"

Brenda wasn't the typical gossip blogger. She was a credentialed journalist, so the question hit hard. The last time they broke up, Ignacio had been lost and used other women's bodies to numb the excruciating pain. That would not be the case this time. This time, he wasn't a fool. The relationship wasn't real, and he knew Delta didn't care about him.

"No one can predict the future, but we're happy and taking our relationship one day at a time." He and Delta took a moment to look into each other's eyes.

No doubt their "mutual adoration" would play well on camera. Their affection was manufactured for the audience, but he nonetheless experienced a tightening in his chest.

Brenda nodded her satisfaction at the answer. "I heard a

rumor that you're using your downtime between movies to shop the next indie film you're directing. Is it true?"

The Entertainment Report had been purchased by Brockwell Media, a film production company based in Atlanta, which was why Ignacio hadn't hesitated to stop and talk to Brenda. If he played his cards right, a little goodwill could go a long way in this instance.

"Your sources are correct," he said with a humble laugh. "The film is titled *Wrong*. It's very personal to me and loosely based on a family story."

"Interesting. Will you be starring in it?"

"No, I'll be behind the camera."

"Well, I wish you the best with your passion project. I know you'll knock it out of the park. Delta, how is that album coming?"

"I'm in the studio working hard every day," Delta replied.

"Do you have a release date for your fans?"

"Not yet. I'm a perfectionist, and I won't release the album until it's where it should be. I owe my fans that much." Looking into the camera, Delta touched her chest to show her heartfelt sincerity. "Be patient with me. I promise you'll love it."

"I'm a Delta J fan myself, so I'm looking forward to your release. Will this album include—"

Rochelle came up behind them. "We have to go," she whispered, nudging them with gentle fingers.

Brenda smiled. "Thank you both very much. Enjoy your evening."

They sauntered away, and Rochelle guided them to their table in the huge ballroom. The luxurious décor included gold chandeliers, sleek black marble floors, and small floral arrangements on each table. The hum of conversation filled the space, punctuated by the occasional burst of laughter from the A-list guests.

As Ignacio helped Delta into her seat, he noticed people watching them. Sitting beside her, he heard her let out a slow, controlled breath.

"That wasn't too bad, was it?" he asked.

"I guess not."

Her voice was neutral, and he couldn't tell if she was serious or being sarcastic.

"How do you think we did?" He slipped an arm along the back of her chair.

"I don't think anyone will have a clue we're being dishonest, if that's what you're asking."

Her bare shoulders shimmered under the soft lights, capturing his attention. All the pretending should have been draining, but Ignacio felt the opposite, as if the touching, brushing against each other, and smelling her perfume had invigorated him. He felt oddly alive, his nerves buzzing with restless energy.

Her full lips parted slightly, as if she had more to say, and a thought entered his head. Completely crazy.

Kiss her.

He remembered how her lips used to feel against his. Petal-soft. So soft he could kiss her for hours and never tire of her succulent mouth. He wanted that experience again.

Right here. Right now.

He leaned closer, and she stiffened. "Go with it," he whispered, brushing his nose along her ear.

Her body remained tense, and she turned slightly toward him. "Ignacio, I don't think—"

He kissed the corner of her mouth, and then, with deliberate slowness, used the tip of his tongue to taste her before capturing her plump bottom lip between his. Her soft mouth yielded to him, and what sounded like an involuntary whimper escaped her.

Ignacio gently tugged on her lip before releasing her. Delta's breathing sounded jagged in his ears. The teasing gesture only lasted for a moment, but he turned rock hard, his pelvis tightening like a clenched fist.

As they looked into each other's eyes, Ignacio wanted to pull her closer and kiss her again, longer this time and more thoroughly, unconcerned if they had an audience.

Then a memory slammed into his brain. A small velvet box. An engagement ring never given. Sitting in the safe at home.

He eased back and removed his arm from the back of her chair. "That should get the tongues wagging," he said, his voice rougher than expected.

"Yeah," Delta replied softly, her eyes downcast.

The lights dimmed, signaling that everyone should take their seats because the ceremony was about to begin. A rapper and his wife sat next to Delta and immediately struck up a conversation.

Meanwhile, the magnitude of what Ignacio had done weighed heavily on his mind. He ran his fingers through his hair as his thoughts raced.

He had done a very foolish thing. He had kissed Delta and tasted heaven on her lips.

And now, he wanted more.

Chapter Eight

"Smoking is bad for your health." The admonishment came from Ignacio's oldest sibling, his stepbrother Ethan.

They sat in front of the fire pit in the backyard of their brother Bruno's house, enjoying the cool fall evening after a delicious meal. Ethan had come straight from work and wore a white shirt that contrasted with his mahogany skin.

"I'm trying to quit." Ignacio dropped the cigarette to the ground and extinguished it with the heel of his shoe.

"I thought you *had* quit." Ethan sipped his after-dinner drink in a relaxed pose.

"I did, sort of. I'm a little stressed, that's all." Ever since Delta showed up at his L.A. condo, and the kiss on Saturday hadn't helped.

"Are you worried about getting funding for the movie?" Ethan asked.

"Yes and no, but I have other issues on my mind."

After the kiss, the evening with Delta had been a blur of performances, speeches, and nonstop interactions with people in the industry. After the limo pulled up in front of her home, they walked to the front door, and he suffered from the disturbing urge to kiss her again.

What the hell was wrong with him? She couldn't be trusted. Eleven goddamn years had passed since their breakup. This should be a cakewalk.

"Ignacio, you have some explaining to do."

His head snapped up at the sound of Bruno's accented voice when he joined them outside. Dark-haired with gray eyes, he was a successful chef and restaurateur recently returned from his honeymoon in Fiji.

Ignacio liked to think the marriage was all thanks to him, considering he was the one who had suggested Bruno hire a matchmaking service to find a wife. Then he and his matchmaker ended up falling in love.

"What are you talking about?" Ignacio asked.

Bruno stopped beside his chair. "This," he said, showing his phone screen.

Ignacio groaned inwardly when he saw the headline. *Ignacio Santana and Delta J Made Their Red Carpet Debut at the Black and Gold Music Experience.*

The drama was about to start, and he hadn't figured out an explanation for his family yet.

"Oh, that," he said in a nonchalant tone.

"Yes, that."

"Since when do you follow online gossip?"

He had expected that, if his relationship with Delta came up, it would be due to his sister Monica—a social media influencer who practically lived online. But his family didn't typically pay attention to tabloid stories about him. They had grown used to the rumor mill surrounding his life over the years and knew better than to believe anything in print unless he confirmed the story himself.

"I don't consider this story about you and Delta to be the usual tabloid gossip. Explain yourself." Bruno sat in the chair between Ignacio and Ethan.

"Delta?" Ethan repeated.

Bruno showed him the phone, and Ethan's eyebrows shot up.

"Tell me this is one of those fake news stories," he said.

Before Ignacio could answer, the back door opened, and their brother Thiago came out with a plate of food and a glass of red wine.

"You finally decided to join us," Ignacio said, hoping to divert attention from his situation.

"And I'm starving," Thiago said, his voice edged with the unmistakable lilt of their Spanish heritage.

He sat at the table instead of near the fire with them. Everyone said Bruno looked the most like their father, while Ignacio resembled their mother. Thiago happened to have a blend of features from both parents, including his mother's penetrating dark brown eyes.

His beard was longer than usual, indicating he hadn't had much time for grooming lately. He had recently begun the transition to take over as CEO of their father's company and was practically working around the clock, seven days a week. They had to threaten him to join them, and he had still shown up late. With his shirtsleeves rolled up, he looked like he could go for another eight hours.

"What did I miss?"

Bruno quickly brought him up to speed.

"The media often makes up stories, but that looks real. Are you back together with her?" Thiago asked, disapproval heavy in his voice.

Ignacio was tempted to tell his brothers the truth. He trusted them to keep his plans secret, but since he was already viewed as somewhat of a wild child, he didn't need their judgment.

"There's nothing to tell. Delta and I bumped into each other at the event and took some photos together."

"Bullshit," all three of his brothers said at once.

"What do you mean?" Ignacio said, forcing a laugh.

Thiago swirled the wine in his glass. "You're a good actor, and you sound very convincing, but you and Delta have history. What is going on?"

Ignacio didn't want to lie again, but if Delta was adhering to the deal of only disclosing to a small number of people, he needed to as well. "The three of you are paranoid."

"Here's another article, this time by *The Entertainment Report*, a reputable magazine," Bruno said, looking at his phone. "Ignacio Santana's next leading lady is none other than Delta J, his ex. The couple arrived together at the Black and Gold Music Experience holding hands and looking very much in love as they posed together on the red carpet. How did the two reconcile? They won't say, but it might have something to do with living in the same city for the time being. Ignacio is in Atlanta shopping his independent film, *Wrong*, and Delta is working on her next album, release date to be determined. Looks like the couple's on-again, off-again relationship is officially on—after more than a decade." He stopped reading and looked at Ignacio. "Should I continue?"

"Not necessary," Ignacio said in a dry tone.

Bruno continued nonetheless. "The couple was seen displaying major PDA at their table inside the Astoria Grand Hotel where the ceremony took place, both of them oblivious to the rest of the world around them."

I wouldn't call it major PDA, Ignacio thought.

"Do you think we are idiots? How long did you plan to hide your relationship from us?" Thiago asked.

"You swore you'd never have anything to do with her again," Ethan reminded him.

"I meant it at the time," Ignacio muttered. He wasn't a glutton for punishment.

"What changed?"

He sighed. "If I tell you something, you each have to promise not to say a word to anyone. Not even your wives." He looked pointedly at Bruno and Ethan. "Do I have your word?"

"Yes," they all said.

Ignacio blew out a breath. "Delta and I aren't really back together. We need each other to generate publicity. Me, for my movie, and her for her album."

Bruno's eyebrows drew together. "Are you saying what I think you're saying? This whole thing is a publicity stunt?" he demanded.

"Don't think of it as a stunt. Think of it as—"

"Lying? Being dishonest?" Thiago supplied around a mouthful of food.

"As if you have any problem being dishonest to get what you want," Ignacio said.

"That's different. It's business."

"This is business," Ignacio insisted.

Ethan stared at him. "I'm not sure which is worse—getting back together with her or pretending to get back together with her. You should never be involved with any woman who hurt you." He spoke with vehemence, no doubt because of the misery he suffered at the hands of his ex-wife.

"You don't need to worry about me. I have everything under control." *Except my libido,* he silently added. The worst part was that he and Delta had agreed not to be involved with anyone else, so all he had for relief was his hand.

"We can invest in your movie if that's what you need," Ethan offered.

"I know, and I appreciate it, but I want to do this on my own. I messed up last time."

"Not every investment works out. I've had failed ventures," Bruno pointed out.

"But most of what you've done has succeeded. The only time I tried to do something on my own, it failed, and Father lost money. I don't want to ask him for help again, and I don't want to ask any of you, either."

"That's what family is for—to bear the burden."

"I know," Ignacio said, grateful. "But I need to do this on my own. I *want* to do this on my own."

"Why are you so adamant that you don't need help?" Thiago demanded.

"Because..." Ignacio paused, loath to admit the real reason he was so insistent on finding his own investors and successfully getting his movie made. He stared into the flickering flames. "I haven't done anything on my own since I entered this business. Father is the reason I have a career in Hollywood."

"You're a great actor. You're a natural," Bruno said.

"I started acting when I was five, in a movie with our parents," Ignacio reminded his brother. "Sure, I'm a good actor—hell, an excellent one. But it doesn't change the fact that the last name Santana opened doors. I'm appreciative of the films I've done—from action flicks to dramas to indie films. But I want to try something different, and this story has been eating at me for years. I screwed up with my directorial debut because my heart wasn't in it. But this—this I'm passionate about, and I want to do it on my own—to know I *can* do it. Do you understand? *Wrong* could be the beginning of a different path in my career, but no one will be willing to invest in future projects if I crowdsource the funds from my family—again."

The men fell silent as they digested his words.

"So you and Delta are working together, so to speak. You scratch her back, and she scratches yours," Ethan said.

"Exactly."

"All well and good from the business aspect, but what about the personal aspect?"

"What do you mean?"

"You were smoking earlier. Is this relationship already stressing you out? Can you handle being around your ex?" Ethan asked.

"Of course. Delta and I broke up eleven years ago. I was younger and... foolish. I won't make the same mistake again."

Bruno and Ethan exchanged glances.

"Don't do that. I can handle Delta."

"How long are the two of you supposed to fake being in love?" Thiago asked, slicing into his steak.

"We anticipate no more than six months," Ignacio replied.

"Six months?" Ethan exclaimed.

"That's a long goddamn time," Thiago said.

Bruno shook his head.

"What's the next step?" Thiago asked.

Ignacio hesitated. "We move in together."

A series of dismayed groans filled the yard.

"Thank you for believing in me," Ignacio said dryly.

"Let me guess—while you're living together, you can't see anyone else, right?" Ethan asked.

"Right."

"This should be interesting." Thiago chuckled heartily, something he rarely did.

"Maybe we should place bets on how long he lasts before he's sleeping with the woman he swore he'd never have anything to do with again," Bruno suggested.

"I bet ten grand he doesn't last more than two months. By Thanksgiving, she'll have a ring through his nose," Thiago said.

Ethan chuckled. "I'll give him the benefit of the doubt and suggest twelve weeks. Bruno?"

"I was going to say twelve weeks too, so I'll say thirteen weeks."

"Again, thank you for the vote of confidence, my dear brothers," Ignacio grated. "I might as well join in. I bet ten grand that she and I will spend the entire six months in a platonic relationship, and nothing—" He broke off when all three of his brothers started laughing. "Really?"

"I don't want to take your money, but please, keep us updated on how your relationship is going," Thiago said.

"The only reason you're so cynical is because the closest you've come to a relationship is your job." Thiago scowled at Ignacio. "As for the two of you, you're both married and have forgotten that not everyone wants to be tied down in a relationship. Some of us prefer to be free."

"We'll see how free you'll be in twelve weeks, maybe less." Ethan lifted his glass to his lips.

Ignacio ignored him, and as his brothers turned to other subjects, he doubled down on his determination. He would not give in to Delta James. She had betrayed him once. He'd be a fool to let her back into his life—in any real way—again.

The kiss on Saturday was a fluke. A moment of weakness. He was stronger than they thought, and she held absolutely no power over him.

Chapter Nine

"We're here." Ignacio slowed to a stop behind the real estate agent's black Mercedes.

Thank goodness, Delta thought. As far as she was concerned, the other houses had been a bust.

The agent's vehicle had come to a standstill beside a guard's gate at the entrance to Briarwood Heights, an affluent neighborhood that attracted celebrities and business moguls. The other houses they had visited had also been in gated communities, a very important feature for Ignacio. He had mentioned that ever since an incident with an obsessed fan entering his home, he had been more cautious about having security around him and living in a secure location.

The gate opened, and the guard waved them through.

They had already spent three hours touring homes in Buckhead. Delta couldn't tell if Ignacio liked any of them, as he kept his communication to head nods and soft grunts. If she were his agent, she wouldn't have a clue if her client was pleased or not.

She herself had been less than thrilled by the options, but since she wasn't paying for the rental and would be moving out as soon as their ruse was over, she had withheld her negative opinions. Unlike Ignacio, she smiled and nodded when the agent pointed out appealing features.

Ignacio's red Corvette crawled slowly through the streets. Each home was uniquely designed and surrounded by lush greenery, with lawns spread out before them like carpets. Finally, they arrived at a large Mediterranean-style home in a cul-de-sac. With the exterior made of neutral stucco, the house featured arched windows and imposing solid wood double doors at the front.

Ignacio climbed out of the car, and she watched him as he walked around to the front. He wore loose-fitting jeans and a black long-sleeved Brunello Cucinelli T-shirt, the fabric fitting snugly across his broad chest and highlighting his biceps. A black ring adorned his forefinger, and a black cuff encircled his wrist. His brown and blond curls were effortlessly combed into a high-low style.

She had fashioned her own hair into a loose top knot and wore burgundy joggers with a matching sweatshirt. They had both agreed casual dress made them seem like any other couple searching for a place on a Saturday afternoon. It gave the impression that they were comfortable with each other, which was important when the photos were splashed inside magazines and across the Internet.

Ignacio opened her door, his mouth curving into the kind of smile that melted hearts on-screen and stole breaths in real life. Her mind drifted to the kiss last weekend—an undeniable erotic experience she couldn't forget. The way he had gently tugged her lower lip... teasing, making her wet, making her ache to sit on his face and have his probing tongue slide across her swollen clit.

Casually, he took her hand, and electricity sizzled beneath Delta's skin. They had already touched several times today at the other houses they looked at, yet she hadn't become accustomed to his touch. His hand was warm. Firm. Possessive. Exactly the type of message they wanted to convey to their audience of one.

Delta exited the vehicle, her breath hitching in her throat when she looked into his eyes—gray eyes that held hers captive. His gaze dipped to her lips and lingered long enough to make her knees soften in betrayal.

Be strong, girl.

The spell broke when Mandy Howard, the agent, approached them. Delta blinked and turned to the older woman.

"This way," Mandy said, with a charming Southern accent.

Her rust-red hair barely touched her shoulders. She wore a lightweight teal coat over her dress and a tasteful amount of gold jewelry.

As they approached the door, Delta was acutely aware of Ignacio's hand around hers. It felt... comfortable. Dangerously comfortable. She was playing a part but worried she was walking into a blazing fire, which had been waiting to consume her ever since her father led her up the elevator to Ignacio's condo.

Clutching a notepad to her chest, Mandy pointed to the left. "There's a three-car garage with additional parking in a detached garage in the back. The house sits on an acre lot. With all the trees and shrubbery, you'll have plenty of privacy without feeling isolated. What do you think so far?"

"Very nice," Delta said, impressed by the meticulously landscaped front yard and the manicured hedges lining the circular driveway. The entire house was set back from the street, partially hidden by trees that only allowed a glimpse of the driveway and a peek at the second story.

Ignacio kept his opinion to himself but nodded, suggesting he agreed with Delta's assessment.

"We can walk around outside in a bit. The property has a top-notch security system with cameras. Something the two of you need to keep out the paparazzi and the crazies, I'm sure." Mandy laughed. "Now let's take a look at the gorgeous interior. Right this way."

She opened the front door and gestured for them to precede her inside. Still holding hands, they walked through the interior.

"It's been empty for a couple of months since the last tenant moved out. The owners live overseas and are anxious to rent it, so if there's anything you don't like, let me know, and I'm sure we can negotiate a concession," Mandy said.

She took them into the kitchen, where there were quartz countertops and high-end appliances polished to a shine. A ceiling-mounted wrought-iron pot rack hung above the massive island with an assortment of stainless steel and copper cookware, adding to the kitchen's gourmet feel.

For the first time today, Delta experienced an awakening, as if she had just woken up from a long overdue nap. Her lips slightly parted in awe.

The home she had purchased in Buckhead years ago was nice, but it wasn't really her style. Her father had convinced her to buy it—calling the purchase a good deal at the time. And it was, sold well below market value. But she had never *loved* the property. She could actually see herself living happily in *this* house, with its elegant arches and tile floor. She imagined sipping wine on one of the barstools while a pot of sauce simmered on the stovetop.

Mandy opened the French doors, and they stepped onto the terrace, where Delta drew an impressed breath. Chairs were arranged in front of an outdoor fireplace, and beyond, a white stone path wound through the garden, where a few lingering roses adorned the bushes.

"You don't have the full effect now because it's fall, but during the spring, the garden is filled with roses and creeping jasmine that fill the air with their scent. It's quite lovely," Mandy said.

Delta relinquished Ignacio's hand and ran her fingers along one of the sturdy columns on the terrace. She imagined sitting on the bench down the path and enjoying the sun or simply picking flowers to place in a vase that would rest on the island in the kitchen. If Ignacio didn't want this place, she might be tempted to rent it herself.

"Do you swim?" Mandy asked.

"We do," Ignacio replied.

"Well, you'll appreciate this." She led them to the huge kidney-shaped pool containing a waterslide and surrounded by flagstone decking, with a covered hot tub nearby. Loungers and a table with additional chairs were neatly arranged to make the space a dream for relaxing.

"Doesn't that look like fun?" Mandy asked, her eyes sparkling.

Ignacio's gaze met Delta's. "I can imagine her lounging poolside in one of her bikinis," he said.

Delta's cheeks heated at the comment. If she didn't know better, she'd believe he meant that.

Mandy looked away, as if giving them privacy. Little did she know, this was all for show.

Back inside, they strolled through the open-concept living room with a two-sided fireplace and exposed wooden beams above. The floor-to-ceiling windows gave an unobstructed view of the outdoors, which meant she'd have a great view of the garden when spring arrived—well, she wouldn't be here that long.

The rest of the floor included a half bath, a separate dining room, and a bonus room. There was a gym and media room one floor down, as well as an in-law suite that would allow Ignacio's live-in housekeeper to have her own space. The media room contained sizable plush seating, and Mandy pointed out that it contained a state-of-the-art sound system.

"You could conduct private screenings here if you like," the agent pointed out. "Now for you to see the upstairs. There are five bedrooms, five baths, and a bonus room upstairs. The master suite is to *die* for."

Knots tightened in Delta's stomach in anticipation of seeing the room, but Mandy led them to the other rooms and bathrooms first before she took them to the end, where double doors opened into the primary suite.

"This is the kind of place where you can unwind after a long day," Mandy said.

The room was empty of furniture, but Delta envisioned a king-sized bed, dressers, and other items in the expansive space. What she saw, she loved, including an area with a built-in bookshelf, where she could place a chaise lounge and turn the space into a cozy reading nook.

There was a fireplace made of sleek marble and stone, perfect for chilly winter nights and falling asleep to its warmth as the flames flickered and cast shadows throughout the room.

"His and hers closets," Mandy said, pointing.

Then she led them onto the private balcony where a sliding glass door opened to a seating area with the pool and garden visible below. Natural light poured in through the large windows, and Mandy demonstrated how the motorized blackout curtains worked.

"Heated floors in the bathroom. I forgot to mention the floors in the kitchen are heated too." She strolled across the carpeted floor and pushed open the door to the bathroom.

Inside was a huge shower with a bench and dual rainfall showerheads, as well as a separate jetted tub in front of a frosted window.

"This is lovely," Delta breathed.

"You like it?" She heard the excitement in the agent's voice.

"I love it. Everything about this place is... exceptional... calming." Yes, that was the word she was looking for.

Then she caught herself and froze.

What am I doing?

Choosing this house wasn't her decision to make. Sure, she'd spend time there over the next few months because of her agreement with Ignacio, but they were looking for a place for him. *He* had to love it, and so far she couldn't tell if he did or not.

"Mr. Santana?" Mandy prompted, her expression hopeful.

"Do you mind giving us a moment alone?" Ignacio asked.

"Certainly. Take all the time you need." Mandy left the bedroom and quietly closed the door behind her.

Ignacio looked around the room. "Do you like this house?"

"It's gorgeous."

"So you could see yourself living here?" His gaze rested on her. She had the impression her answer was important to him.

"Sure. Not just living here but being inspired here. I love the serenity of the location."

"We should rent it, then."

"We?"

"I like it too."

"But it's your decision. You have to live here," Delta pointed out.

"So will you, and if you're like me, you weren't very impressed with the other options."

"True." She would love living here and hate to leave after the pretense was over, but until then, there was nothing wrong with enjoying herself. "I like it. You like it, and there's plenty of space so we won't be in each other's way."

He stiffened, an odd expression crossing his face. "Wouldn't want that," he muttered, hooking his thumbs in his belt loops. "Let's let Mandy know."

Without waiting for a reply, he yanked open the door.

If Delta didn't know better, she'd think she had pissed him off.

Chapter Ten

Ignacio Santana and Delta J Were Spotted House Hunting in Atlanta
Wedding Bells Soon?

Holding his phone, Ignacio stared at the headline and accompanying photos from several days ago. Living with Delta was either the smartest or dumbest move he had ever made in his life. He hadn't decided yet.

He went over to the window and peered down at the front of the house. He had moved in several days ago and watched a small army of men unload Delta's clothes and furniture and carry them into the house. How much stuff did she have?

He left the room and walked down the hall. The men called out to each other, and he also heard Delta's voice, softer and more measured as she directed them on where to take the boxes they brought in from the truck.

Passing by the open door of the primary suite, he spotted

containers and luggage on the floor near the bed. They'd be sleeping in that room together every night.

For six months.

Ignacio rubbed tension from the back of his neck. He needed a cigarette but fought valiantly against the urge. At least the publicity was already paying off, and he'd find out how much during the scheduled meeting with his manager and assistant in a few minutes.

He entered the office he had set up in the bonus room. Crystal, his assistant, glanced over her shoulder at him when he came in. In her late twenties, she had worked with him for several years now. Her glasses, casual clothes, and perpetual bun fooled people into thinking she was a pushover, but she was far from it. More like a pit bull.

She was an integral part of his team, not only because she ran his errands and made "anonymous" phone calls to alert the media to his whereabouts from time to time. She was also his first line of defense with fans. She went through his mail, checking for outrageous requests and declarations of love. Anything deemed out of the ordinary or hinting at danger was turned over to the authorities—a thankfully rare occurrence.

Every few months she threatened to leave him based on some request she deemed extreme, but she hadn't yet, and he knew why. She loved a challenge.

"What do you have for me?" Ignacio asked, taking a seat behind his glass-topped desk.

Other than the chairs, it was the only furniture in the room. The walls were bare, but Crystal would make the place look livable soon enough. Or would Delta? He'd only expected her to bring clothes, but the movers had already unloaded a few pieces of furniture.

Crystal lowered her gaze to the tablet in her hand, using the electronic pen to scroll through her list. "I have mostly good news. Here are some of the headlines: *Are Ignacio Santana and Delta J the Country's Hottest Romance?*"

"The hottest in the country?" Ignacio repeated with a laugh. Despite being in the entertainment industry for years, he had never gotten accustomed to the hyperbole used to sell magazine copies and prompt clicks.

Crystal shrugged and continued.

From Teenage Sweethearts to Hollywood's Hottest Reunion —Ignacio & Delta Are Back, Baby!

Sorry Ladies, Ignacio Santana is Off the Market, Thanks to Delta J

Caught on Camera! Hollywood Heartthrob Ignacio Santana and R&B Songstress Delta J Are Giving Love Another Try

Inside Ignacio Santana and Delta J's Sudden Reconnection

"That one lists insider sources as having the scoop," Crystal explained.

"Of course," Ignacio said dryly.

"Nothing too scandalous though. Basically, that the two of you have moved into a home in a gated community in Atlanta, blah, blah, blah. A couple of photographs of you going into one of the houses and pulling up to the front gate here."

She showed him the pictures, and he took a moment to examine them. Delta looked great, as was to be expected. The top knot showed off the graceful lines of her neck, and the joggers hugged her ass and showed off her delicious curves. Feeling his blood heat up, Ignacio thrust the tablet back at Crystal.

"What else?" he asked in a gruff voice.

Crystal didn't seem to notice. "Here's where it gets interesting." She made eye contact with him, silently telling him to get ready, and he braced himself.

PR Stunt or Lovers Reunited? Inside Ignacio and Delta's Rekindled Love Affair

From Heartbreak to Headlines: The Explosive Return of Ignacio Santana & Delta J's Romance!

"And the last one is... *He Left Her Once—Will He Do It Again? Ignacio & Delta's Shocking Reunion!*"

"Of course they would think I was the one who left," Ignacio muttered.

"You didn't?" Crystal arched an eyebrow.

His breakup with Delta occurred long before Crystal started working for him, and despite their close relationship, he had never told her what happened. There had never been any need to, and he didn't plan to start now.

"No comment." He gave her one of his practiced red carpet smiles to soften the words. "Is that all?"

Knowing better than to continue prying, Crystal moved on. "Those are the most interesting ones. Not too bad, and nothing harmful in any of them that you'd need to take a look at. I already talked to Liz, and she's not worried," Crystal said, referring to his publicist.

He was about to speak when the laptop screen beeped and flickered to life.

"Hey, anybody there?" Yvonne's face appeared on the screen. A light-skinned Black woman with freckles, she currently wore her shoulder-length brown hair secured at the nape. Her brown eyes squinted at the screen, and Ignacio turned on the camera.

"There you are," she said, smiling and sitting back in her chair. "I see Crystal is there too."

"Hey, Yvonne." Crystal waved.

"Hi, honey. How's it going?"

"Keeping this man straight, as usual."

"It's more than a full-time job, isn't it?"

"Who you telling?"

They cackled.

"Very funny, ladies." Ignacio crumpled a Post-it note and tossed it at Crystal's head.

She batted away the paper and glared at him. "How's the hubby?" she asked.

Yvonne had been happily married to her high school sweetheart for almost forty-three years.

"We're giving our kids a break and keeping the grandkids over the Christmas holidays, and he's already started making all kinds of improvements to the house." She quietly laughed, shaking her head.

"All four grandkids?" Ignacio asked.

"Yes."

"The holidays are two months away," Crystal said.

"You know how my husband is. He likes to be prepared, and I'm not going to bother him. Projects keep him busy and happy, and if he's happy, so am I."

Ignacio considered their marriage one to be admired. They were both deeply in love and happy to have found each other and stayed together all these years. He and Delta could have done the same, but....

Shaking off the thought, he pushed it aside.

"Okay, down to business," Yvonne said. "I have great news. I received a call from Brockwell Media."

Ignacio straightened in his chair, and so did Crystal.

Yvonne was grinning from ear to ear. "They want to invest in your film."

"No fucking way. Yvonne, are you serious?" Ignacio asked.

"I would not kid about something like this. I know how much you've been wanting to make this film happen, and they are *very* interested."

Crystal squealed and danced in her chair, while Ignacio pumped his fist. If Brockwell Media signed on, then other investors would be willing to sign on too.

"They want to meet with you as soon as possible. I checked your calendar, and it looks like you have an opening next Tuesday and one on Thursday. Which one should—"

"Tuesday, of course," Ignacio immediately said.

"Crystal, can you get a proposal to them before then?" Yvonne asked.

"I will hand-deliver it myself," his assistant vowed.

Ignacio sat back in amazement. "This is happening." Finally, after dealing with doubts because of the lack of interest in his project, the tide was turning.

"It's happening," Yvonne confirmed. She flipped a page on her pad and checked her notes. "Your meeting is with the oldest son, King Brockwell. He wants to meet with you privately first. He works very closely with his father, but this project is his baby."

"You make it sound like a done deal," Ignacio said.

"I shared the movie premise, and he loved it. He's looking to forge his own path in the company, and your film is his way to do that."

"What do you need from me?" Ignacio asked.

"Nothing, except make sure you're on time on Tuesday. Crystal...?"

"I'm on it, don't worry, he'll be early," Crystal assured her.

They spent the next few minutes discussing the details before Yvonne had to go. When she was gone, Ignacio turned to Crystal, who wore a huge grin on her face.

"This is amazing!" she exclaimed.

Chuckling, Ignacio stood. "I know, but I don't want to get too excited. One step at a time. We get the proposal in King's hands, and then we go from there."

"I have absolutely no doubt they'll finance the movie. It's a great story." She had been one of the few people he let read an early draft of the script. Crystal checked her watch. "I'm on my way to the store to pick up your snacks, and then I'll work on the proposal package when I get back."

"Did you—"

"Yes, I already printed out the NDAs for the new staff. The landscapers will arrive on Monday afternoon. I'll show them around and get them to sign the agreement. Maria won't arrive until Wednesday, by the way, which means you're on your own for meals until then. Do you want me to check into a food service for you and Delta?"

"No, that's not necessary. We can figure out our meals until Maria gets here. I might even do some cooking."

"Ooh, that'll be nice. Put in some work in that beautiful kitchen. If you make your grandmother's chicken mole, you better save me some."

"When have I ever not saved you some?"

She grinned. "Just making sure. Alrighty, I'm heading out. Later." She saluted and left him alone.

Ignacio lingered behind in the office, listening to the distant sound of the men moving through the house, bringing in Delta's belongings.

Delta.

He used to keep her updated on all his wins and losses, and each time he had professional success and signed a contract or booked a gig, she celebrated. He had done the same for her.

He had a sudden urge to share his good news with her.

But things were different now, and there was animosity between them instead of friendship and affection.

Would she even care?

Chapter Eleven

The house was much quieter since the movers had gone.

Delta placed her blouses in the dresser and shut the drawer. When she turned around, Ignacio was standing in the doorway, arms folded across his chest.

Her skin prickled under his gaze. "Hey."

"Don't you have someone who can do that for you?" he asked, inclining his head toward the rest of the clothes in the open suitcases on the bed.

"I like doing some things myself."

They hadn't seen much of each other today. He had been in his office most of the time, leaving once to go out while she worked with the movers. When he returned, he brought back Indian food and explained that his housekeeper, Maria, wouldn't arrive from California until next Wednesday. Until then, they were on their own.

She studied his face, the neat scruff of hair on his jawline, and the pointed tip of his nose. He wasn't just handsome. He was charismatic, exuding a confidence that made him even more attractive. What choice did he have but to become a movie star? If he hadn't, the world would have been robbed of his persona.

"I was thinking, since we're alone in the house tonight, I'll sleep in the spare bedroom," Ignacio said.

"Oh?"

"We don't need to share a bed until Maria gets here."

Share a bed. Hearing those words made her nerve endings tingle.

"Makes sense," Delta said.

There was a moment of awkward silence.

"We're going to have to learn to live together like normal people and act normal around the staff," Ignacio said.

"I'll do my best, but you're the actor, remember?" She continued putting away her clothes, walking from the bed to the dresser and back again.

"You're angry," he said.

Delta tossed the pants she was holding back into the suitcase. "Aren't you? Don't you hate putting on this charade when you have a million things to do?"

"Believe me, I don't like doing this any more than you do."

It was probably particularly difficult for him, given that his name had been linked with numerous women over the years: models, actresses, socialites, unknowns. He didn't discriminate, and he was not known for being monogamous.

"What's going on with your album?" Ignacio asked.

The question surprised her. They didn't talk much when they were alone or show any interest in each other's projects, as if conversation was too much of a burden without an audience.

"Dad wants me in the studio tomorrow, so that's where I'll be."

"No rest for the weary."

"Never," she said ruefully. "I... I'm having a bit of a hard time. None of the music feels right. The songs the label provided don't move me."

Ignacio leaned his shoulder against the doorframe, settling in for the conversation. "Do you still write?"

He was probably remembering her notebooks filled with poetry and love songs she'd shown him when they were teenagers. She had held on to them all, though she never planned for anyone else to see them. Some were good, some were bad, but overall, compared to her work now, her growth as an artist was clear.

"A little," she admitted.

"A little?"

"Okay, I have dozens of songs written," she confessed.

She had written songs the label had passed on to other singers, several of which continued to generate good money due to the success of the artists singing the lyrics. But most of the songs she had kept to herself.

"If you have dozens, why don't you use some of them?"

Delta laughed shortly. "They don't want those songs. They're too angsty."

"Have you asked?" He raised his right eyebrow.

"No," Delta admitted in a low voice.

"Then you don't know that they don't want your songs. I remember you wrote some good poetry."

"You're a liar," she muttered.

Ignacio's eyebrows snapped together. "What did you say?"

"You're a liar," Delta said louder.

"You don't believe me?"

"I bet you don't remember a single line from one of my poems."

He didn't say a word at first, and she watched him defiantly, daring him to contradict her. Then he spoke.

"Flowers blooming through the frost
Hearts dare beat though all is lost
Love is passion, love is pain
Love is sunshine, love is rain"

"Th-that's my poem, Love Is. How did you... I don't understand. You remembered that?"

"Of course I remembered it. It was beautiful. Angsty. Emotional." Ignacio began reciting the rest of the verses, and all Delta could do was stare. At the end, she joined him in repeating the last two lines.

"Love is passion, love is pain. Love is sunshine, love is rain." She drew in a tremulous breath, shocked and overwhelmed. "I wrote that in tenth grade."

"You wrote it our junior year," Ignacio corrected.

Delta paused. "Oh my goodness, you're right!" She laughed. He remembered better than she did. "I can't believe..."

"I told you, you write good stuff. You need to believe in yourself, Delta."

She bit the inside of her cheek. "You're right. But I'm not as confident about my skills as you are, I guess."

Imposter syndrome. She had learned the phrase years ago in therapy and had come to better understand those feelings of inadequacy and the belief that she didn't deserve her status in the industry. Her last album flopping certainly didn't help.

He had been self-assured, even when they were teenagers in the performing arts club in middle school. Because of her good grades, she had won a scholarship to attend the prestigious Westerly Academy, where the wealthy and notable people in Atlanta sent their kids. That's where they had become close.

He never seemed to have doubts, and at times, that rubbed other kids the wrong way. They had called him egotistical and conceited, but none of the disparaging words had affected him. He knew he was good at his craft, and if anything, while they whined and complained, he worked hard to be better.

"I'm not always confident," Ignacio admitted. "But I remind myself that if I don't believe in myself, why should anyone else?" He shrugged.

"That's one way to look at it," Delta murmured. "What about you? How is your film project coming along? Is the script finalized?"

"More or less. Do you know what the movie is about?"

"Vaguely."

She knew more about his first film because she had seen it. Though panned by critics, she didn't think it was that bad, especially for a directorial debut.

"I got the idea from something that happened to a family member," Ignacio explained.

That much Delta knew, but this was the most they had talked, and she was curious to know more. "So it's inspired by true events?"

"Not exactly. The true event gave me the idea, the way you might get an idea for a song from something you see or experience. What you're singing might not be based in fact, but the story in the lyrics could stem from something that really happened. One of my father's cousins in Mexico was convicted of a murder he didn't commit. When he was released, he continued to insist he hadn't killed the man, but no one believed him."

"Because he'd always been in trouble," Delta guessed.

"Yes. Yet he was adamant he hadn't done it, and my father, being my father, eventually looked into the case and discovered discrepancies."

She wasn't surprised. On the occasions she had met Benicio Santana, he had seemed like an honorable man, though rather strict. He had imposed a lot of restrictions on Ignacio at the start of his career.

Ignacio was not allowed to participate in events unless Benicio or another adult family member was present. Meanwhile, Delta's parents allowed her to hang out in spaces a minor shouldn't have been. Looking back, their lack of oversight was reckless, but at the time, she and Ignacio had fumed about his father's overprotectiveness.

"Eventually, my father hired a private investigator, and she did some digging and found out his cousin was wrongfully convicted."

Her eyes widened. "Stories like that always horrify me. How long was he imprisoned?"

"Fifteen years."

Delta gasped in dismay. "Thank goodness for your father."

He nodded slowly. "He was able to clear his cousin's name and then set him up with whatever he wanted to do. His cousin, Carlo, chose to create a nonprofit to help formally incarcerated people transition back into society. He knew it would have been impossible for him without my father's help."

"Which parts of his life did you use to inspire your film?" Delta asked. The movie was more intriguing now that she knew what had sparked the idea for the project.

"The wrongful conviction and the time he spent in jail," he answered, shifting against the door. "At the end of the movie, the character, Gideon, also sets up a nonprofit, but that's where the similarities end. The story takes place here in the States, not Mexico. Gideon is played by a white guy—a new actor I discovered at a local theater. As soon as I saw him, I knew he'd be perfect for the part. The man is amazing, and his audition blew everyone away. When the character comes out of jail, he finds out he has a son with the woman he was involved with before his incarceration."

"She never told him he had a kid?" Delta asked.

Ignacio shook his head. "They were from opposite sides of the tracks, different social classes. He was a poor kid, smart and on his way to college on a scholarship when he was arrested. She is the daughter of a wealthy philanthropist and currently runs the family foundation. She ends up helping her ex at the risk of destroying her reputation and having everyone find out this criminal is the father of her son."

"What does she risk?" Delta asked.

"Alienating her family and losing donors."

She paused, thinking about the story in her head. She was already intrigued and saw how it could play out on screen. "Do they fall in love?"

"They do, as she starts to work on his case to help him. Their feelings for each other cause problems because she's now married to a well-known politician running for state senator. He's been great and is a father figure to her son."

"Sounds messy, but a romance subplot is always a nice touch." She noticed him frowning. "What's wrong?"

He shrugged. "I don't know. The script is complete, but it needs tweaking. I feel as if there's something missing, but I don't know what it is."

"What feedback have you gotten from other people?"

"Everyone who has read it loves the script, but I... I don't know," he finished, sounding exasperated.

"Maybe you're overthinking it," Delta said gently. She understood because she could get inside her own head sometimes. He didn't want to fail again, just as she didn't want her next album to flop.

"Maybe. Brockwell Media reached out," Ignacio said.

"Who are they?"

"The biggest production company in the South. If they're interested and sign on, the movie is as good as done."

"Ohmigod! What? That's amazing. Way to bury the lede."

Ignacio chuckled, and the low sound was sexy and enticing. His whole face changed—softening, brightening. Her insides ached with the need to reach out and touch him and bury her fingers in his soft curls. Instead, she buried her fingers in the clothes in her suitcase—a pitiful substitute for what she really wanted to do.

"I meet with them on Tuesday."

Delta noted his tempered reaction. "You should be way more excited than you are," she remarked.

"I don't want to put the cart before the horse," he explained.

"You haven't changed a bit."

"What do you mean?" he asked, sounding offended.

"You don't like to get too excited about good news."

"Because in the blink of an eye, good news can turn into bad news. You know that."

"True." She let out a little laugh.

He tilted his head. "What are you thinking about?"

"That time you auditioned for the soda commercial back in middle school."

He paused, and then his eyes lit up as he remembered. "Oh damn, I forgot about that. I had to pretend to like that awful drink." His upper lip curled in distaste.

"It was so gross." Delta wrinkled her nose. She had been proud of him and insisted her father buy an entire case. "It tasted like carbonated cough medicine."

"Worse. I warned you, but you didn't listen."

"I was certain it couldn't be as bad as you said."

He chuckled, his voice warm at the memory. "I had my first national commercial, only for them to call me the next morning and say, 'We're going in a different direction.'" He shook his head, and his curls tumbled around his face.

"Um, it probably didn't help that you were running through the halls at school singing 'All I Do is Win' by DJ Khaled."

He laughed again. "I did do that, didn't I?"

"Yeah, you did."

"You're right, that probably didn't help."

"Hey, at least you didn't suffer for very long. You landed a shampoo deal a few months later." Because of his beautiful hair and the success of the initial commercial, the brand created a series of commercials that played nationally and elevated his profile.

"Thanks to Yvonne. The exposure changed my life."

Despite their personal conflict, deep down she wanted a win for him, and a small part of her was pleased by the amount of information he'd shared.

Ignacio straightened from the wall. "It's late." He went into the bathroom and came out with his toothbrush.

"That's all you need? Do you have clothes in the spare room?" Delta asked.

"No."

"Then..."

A smirk tucked into the right corner of his mouth.

"You still sleep naked," Delta surmised.

"Yes."

She felt a pull in her belly as memories of his warm, naked body pressed against hers beneath cool sheets came flooding back.

"It's very comfortable. You should try it."

"Do you plan to do the same thing when... when we're in the same bed?" Delta asked.

He paused, watching her closely before answering. "Yes."

"Oh. Okay."

"You have a problem with that?"

"Not a problem for me," she said with a casual shrug.

"Glad to hear it. Good night."

He was gone before she had the presence of mind to respond.

"Good night," she said, her voice a little breathless.

Then she replayed their conversation in her mind and grinned. Ignacio had remembered her poem from eleventh grade. The *whole* poem.

He had shared his success with her, like old times. He had laughed with her—real laughter, not fake. Maybe living together wasn't such a bad idea after all.

And maybe, just maybe, Vivian was right. Maybe Ignacio didn't hate her.

Chapter Twelve

Brockwell Media was a multi-billion dollar holding company with subsidiaries spanning film production, digital and print media, radio, and cable television.

Ignacio straightened his tie as a very attractive assistant escorted him down the hall to King Brockwell's office. After a brief knock, she led him into the room, and King approached right away with his hand extended. As the woman quietly left, both men shook hands.

"Ignacio Santana, nice to meet you," King said.

He was over six feet tall with dark brown skin and low cut hair. He wore a dark suit and a black Rolex on his wrist. With his looks, he could easily be a star in the same movies his family produced.

"Nice to meet you too," Ignacio replied, shaking his hand.

"Please, have a seat." King waved him over to the seating area. "Can I interest you in a drink, or is it too early for that?"

Ignacio eyed the fully stocked bar as he sat down. "Nothing for me, thanks."

King sat across from him. They spent the next few minutes

engaging in small talk, and Ignacio had the impression that King was feeling him out and trying to get a sense of his personality.

Finally, his host steered the conversation toward the business at hand. "I really appreciate you coming in today. I wanted to meet with you one-on-one first before we brought in the team, so I could share my plans and get a sense of your flexibility. My father usually handles the movie deals. That's how this company was founded. He grew this empire from one film."

"Impressive," Ignacio said, though he was already familiar with the story of Brockwell Media and its origins.

"I've worked closely with my father for years, and I'm ready to branch out into movie-making myself, which is why I'm interested in *Wrong*. I'd heard rumors that you were going to make another movie, but I'll be honest, I wasn't interested until I saw a piece about you in one of our magazines—*The Entertainment Report*. Anyway, the article prompted me to do a little research, and that's why I reached out to Yvonne. I received your proposal and read the script. It's exactly the kind of project I've been looking to sink my teeth into—a project that allows me to experiment and take the kind of risks I can't with the mainstream projects we usually acquire.

"*Wrong* has all the elements of an emotional film, the writing is solid, and I appreciate the theme of the wrongful conviction of the main character. Frankly, I think it could be a contender during awards season."

Everything he was saying so far was positive, yet Ignacio sensed a "but" coming.

"But," King said, "I feel as if there's something missing. I'm not a creative person, so I can't pinpoint what that something is. Would you be willing to work with one of our screenwriters to take another look at the script?"

Ignacio paused. This was his baby, but he agreed with

King. There was something missing, and he couldn't figure out what that might be. Another set of eyes, a professional, might be what was needed to get past the niggling doubt about the storyline.

"I'm open to the idea," he said.

"Excellent." A broad grin crossed King's face. "In that case, Brockwell Media would like to produce your film. I want to finance the entire project."

Ignacio, though excited, looked at him with surprise. "Did I hear you correctly?" If Brockwell Media financed the entire project, he wouldn't have to find other investors, which would simplify the production process and potentially lead to a strong partnership, opening up other opportunities if the film was successful.

"You heard me correctly. Do we have a deal?" King extended his hand across the table between them.

Ignacio grabbed his hand and gave it a firm pump. "You said exactly what I wanted to hear."

They shared a laugh.

"Listen, there's one more thing. It's a favor, actually, and I hope you don't mind."

Uh oh. "What is it?"

"My assistant reached out to Delta J's management team to hire her for a party we're having, but she was told Delta doesn't do private engagements. I wouldn't ask if it wasn't important, but I was wondering if you could convince her to perform at this event. It's for my mother's seventieth birthday party. We never thought she'd live to see this particular birthday. She had a cancer scare a year ago."

"I'm sorry to hear that," Ignacio said with sincere sympathy.

"It was rough, believe me. My mother is the soul of our family, and we thought we were going to lose her." King's eyes clouded as he recalled that tough period. "To celebrate, my father is throwing a big bash for her, and frankly, I'm in competition with my brothers to get her the best gift. She's a big fan of Delta J's. She loves her soulful voice. Says it reminds her of her favorite singers from back in the day. What do you think—could you convince her to make an exception this time around?"

"When is the birthday party?"

"Saturday. I know, I know, it's short notice, but I'm willing to pay any price to have Delta J perform. She doesn't have to do a big production. A couple of songs in her beautiful voice will be enough to make my mother happy. I'd love to surprise her with that gift."

"I'll talk to her and see what I can do," Ignacio promised.

"Thank you." King stood, and Ignacio did too.

They strolled to the door, and King opened it. "Again, I appreciate you taking the time to meet with me. I look forward to working with you on *Wrong*. I'll have my people reach out to yours so we can get the ball rolling."

"Sounds good."

When Ignacio entered the house, he was still in a good mood. The meeting with King Brockwell had gone better than expected, but now there was the situation concerning Delta. Though King hadn't suggested the deal hinged on her willingness to sing at his mother's birthday party, having Delta perform certainly wouldn't hurt.

He found her in the kitchen sitting on one of the stools, slathering mustard on wheat bread as she made a ham sandwich.

"That's what you're having for dinner?" Ignacio asked.

"I'm cheating today."

"You're eating a ham sandwich on your cheat day?"

She shrugged, slicing the sandwich in half. "Dad doesn't usually approve of me eating carbs." She bit into the sandwich and closed her eyes, humming with appreciation as if she were eating lobster thermidor.

He understood the need to stay in shape. In between films, he exercised regularly and ate healthy food because his body was as important as his acting skills.

"I eat cake on my cheat day and then exercise harder to offset the extra calories. Which reminds me, Maria arrives tomorrow, and she makes a delicious tres leches cake."

Delta groaned. "Don't. I have a weakness for homemade desserts."

He fought a smile. She looked genuinely tormented by the idea. "I haven't forgotten. Whenever you came to the house, you weren't shy about devouring the pies and cakes my mother made."

"Or the chocolate chip cookies with macadamia nuts. Lawd have mercy." She lifted her hands in silent praise. She turned hopeful eyes to him. "Does she still make them?"

"Not as much as before, but I can make sure you get some."

"You don't have to do that," she said dismissively, almost as if she were embarrassed.

"Maybe I want to." The words slipped from his lips before he realized they were leaving. He froze.

Delta blinked, surprise evident on her face.

"Oh. Well, if you want to." She lifted a shoulder in an adorable one-shoulder shrug.

"I'll put in a good word for you with my mother. I'm sure she won't mind."

"Thank you."

An almost bashful smile touched her lips, and his heart

constricted as he was reminded of that same bashful smile when they met at thirteen in the performing arts club and had to practice their lines together. Even back then, he had been smitten by her beauty—her lovely dark chestnut skin, those beautiful brown eyes with curled lashes, and her hair braided into thin ropes that framed her face. They may have started out as friends, but he had known right away that she was special.

Going down memory lane was dangerous, but Ignacio sensed a shift in their relationship ever since move-in day. They were more relaxed with each other and willing to joke around, and since they both had their own schedules keeping them busy, living in the same house wasn't as terrible as he had thought it would be. He had dreaded seeing her every day and dealing with the constant tension coursing through his body whenever she was near.

Instead, a tentative truce had been established between them. He certainly didn't mind when he heard her humming in the halls or her voice carrying from downstairs to the second floor as she worked with her vocal coach. The sound of her voice was... soothing. He understood why King's mother was a fan.

He went to the stainless-steel refrigerator and removed a small bottle of orange juice. "I need to talk to you about something. I had my meeting with King Brockwell at Brockwell Media today."

"How did it go?" Delta took a bite of her sandwich.

"He wants to do the movie."

Her eyes widened. "For sure? So it's a done deal?"

"Yes. He's financing the whole project."

Her mouth fell open. "That's great! Congratulations!"

He laughed at her genuine enthusiasm. Back in the day, she would have flung her arms around his neck, but this reaction would have to suffice. "Hold on, the details have to be worked out and contracts have to be signed," he said, not only to temper her excitement but his own as well.

"So you've decided not to get too happy?" she asked in a teasing voice.

"You know how I am. But also, he asked me for a favor." Ignacio went into detail about King's request and finished with, "He said he's willing to pay whatever price you want."

Delta frowned. Not the expression he had expected to see on her face.

"It's not about the money," she quickly explained.

"If it's not about the money, why don't you do private parties?" Ignacio asked.

She sighed. "Dad thinks they cheapen my brand."

"Do you agree?" Ignacio sipped from his bottle of orange juice, keeping his eyes on her.

"To a certain extent, but I mean, there *are* plenty of artists who do them and charge a hefty fee."

Ignacio watched her pick at the bread. "Is that the only reason?"

"There was a... security issue once, a long time ago when I used to do them. Ever since then, we've avoided small parties."

"I don't think you have to worry about a security issue with the Brockwells, and I'll be there. We can make sure Ava is there."

"I don't think all that is necessary. Besides, I like the idea of celebrating King's mother's birthday because she overcame cancer. If I did perform at her party, I wouldn't charge. I'll just need to run it by my father. When is the party?"

"This Saturday."

"*This* Saturday?"

He nodded.

Her eyes widened. "That's not very much notice to put together a set."

"King insisted you don't need to do much. I got the impression it'll be a small affair. He just wants to give his mother a nice gift, and that's hearing you sing."

"Do you think your movie hinges on my singing at the party?" Her brow wrinkled.

"I can't say for sure, but it doesn't matter. If you really don't want to perform for the Brockwells, you don't have to. Don't accept the invitation just to make sure my film deal goes through."

"Isn't your film deal the reason we're doing all this?"

"Yes, but I wouldn't want you to be in a situation that makes you uncomfortable or goes against what you normally do in business. It's your career. You make the choice."

Hearing him say those words seemed to alleviate her concerns, and she visibly relaxed.

"It's short notice, but I can practice a few songs to be ready by this Saturday. I need to find out which ones are her favorites." She tapped her chin.

"You're sure you're okay with singing at the party? You're not worried about your father's reaction?"

"He'll be fine," she said dismissively. "He came up with that rule about tarnishing my brand when I was on top of the charts. That's not exactly the case anymore. I'm in."

She bit into her sandwich.

Ignacio drained the last of his orange juice and placed the bottle on the counter. "What happened with the security risk?"

Delta's shoulders tensed, and she shifted in her seat as if she wanted to escape the question. "It was a small group." She started slowly, hesitantly. "Three men and their wives—and one of the guys got handsy. He's the son of a hedge fund owner. Because it was a small group, I didn't have security with me. Just me and the band and Dad. The guy's wife was furious at his behavior, and eventually, Dad hauled him out of the room.

He was obviously drunk and completely out of control. The family ended up paying another twenty-five percent on top of the regular fee for the trouble—and probably to keep the incident quiet."

If Ignacio had been there, he would have done more than drag the man out of the room. The asshole would have taken a fist to the jaw. "You shouldn't have had to put up with that."

"It was nothing."

"I wouldn't call it nothing," Ignacio said.

Eyes downcast, Delta picked up her sandwich and drink. "Compared to other stuff... It was nothing. I'm going to finish my meal upstairs. Congratulations, Ignacio." Her voice ended on a soft note, her words heartfelt.

"Thank you."

She walked out of the kitchen, leaving him to stare after her. He got the impression she was running.

Women in the entertainment industry had to put up with so much shit, and as beautiful as Delta was, he suspected she'd dealt with major dickheads. Men who thought women were property, existing solely for their pleasure. He hated to think she had been subjected to that sort of behavior.

But her words stood out to him, forming a knot of unease in his belly. *Compared to other stuff.*

What other stuff? What the hell had happened?

Chapter Thirteen

You can't stay in here all night.

Delta stared at her reflection in the bathroom mirror, trying to work up the courage to go into the bedroom. She had been in the bathroom ever since she heard Ignacio enter the primary suite while she was getting ready.

What was she afraid of? They were getting along better. The animosity she had experienced from him in L.A. and the cool indifference before moving in had diminished.

She was afraid of herself.

Afraid of how she would behave once she was in bed with Ignacio, tempted by his naked body on the mattress next to hers. She hadn't forgotten the kiss at the Black and Gold Music Experience. On the contrary, she thought about it way more than she should—reliving the teasing tug on her lips and his warm breath fanning her mouth. Each time, a gentle, throbbing ache bloomed between her thighs. Their pleasant conversation yesterday had blurred the lines between them even more, causing her to lower her guard and feel more comfortable around him—to the point where she had almost shared her painful secret.

They hadn't spent much time together since then, both busy with their own work. Early that morning, Ignacio had gone running in the neighborhood. He returned as she was walking downstairs to make breakfast, his shirt wet with sweat and clinging to his broad chest. Tendrils of hair curled around his damp forehead in revolt against the elastic tying his hair back. She fought hard not to gawk at him, smiling briefly as she passed him on the staircase on her way to the kitchen.

In the afternoon, Maria arrived, and Ignacio introduced them to each other. She adored his housekeeper right away, a petite and plump Mexican woman with a friendly personality. Delta knew they would get along fine. Now she was here, however, Delta and Ignacio had to share the same bed.

"You can do this. No big deal," she muttered to herself, smoothing a hand over the cornrows in her hair. She would release the braids in the morning to give her hair a wavy appearance during the interviews her publicist had set up.

With one final tug to straighten her ivory pajamas, Delta turned out the light and exited the bathroom, quietly closing the door behind her. The room was dark but not pitch black.

"I thought you had fallen into the toilet," Ignacio remarked.

She paused to let her eyes adjust to the low light in the room. Then she padded over to the king bed. "I appreciate the concern, but as you can see, I didn't."

She saw him better now, with his arms folded behind his head, his biceps flexed and tufts of dark hair sticking out from his armpits.

How did he manage to look so sexy by simply lying on a bed?

"Pajamas. Those are cute," he said.

"Thanks," Delta replied, knowing full well he was making fun of her. She climbed under the covers.

"I don't remember you wearing pajamas before."

"It's been a long time since we've slept in the same bed," she reminded him. "Besides, the pajamas are a good idea. One of us needs to wear clothes."

"I don't know why you're making such a big deal out of this. You never had any problem being naked in bed after we made love."

"That was different."

Delta lay flat on her back and stared up at the ceiling. She had a feeling she'd have a hard time falling asleep.

"Are you ready for the birthday event at the Brockwells?" Ignacio asked.

"Almost. I have a couple of interviews tomorrow, and then I'll spend the rest of the day practicing. By the way, we should probably post pictures of each other on our Instagram profiles."

"I'm way ahead of you. My publicist has a few posts scheduled already. One of them is the photo Crystal took of the two of us eating in the kitchen. The other gives a partial view of the backyard."

"Perfect. I was thinking about posting pictures of the house too. I might use one or two of the kitchen... maybe with a plate of fruit on the island and *Home Sweet Home* as the caption. I don't know. I'm never really good at those manufactured images. My social media manager will probably come up with something better."

"Sounds good to me."

It was strange talking in such clinical terms about how they planned to generate excitement from their followers.

They were both silent for a few minutes, and in the silence, Delta kept thinking about Ignacio being nude under the covers.

The idea of him fully unclothed turned her on, and the fact that she wasn't immune to him annoyed her.

She twisted her head in his direction. "Are you really naked under there?"

Ignacio shifted so he was also looking at her. "What's the problem? I told you before that I still sleep naked."

"There's no problem. I was just wondering about your ass being in the sheets. That's definitely your side of the bed from now on."

"You should free yourself from the confines of clothes and let your ass be in the sheets too."

"I'm good, thanks."

His voice lowered with a hint of amusement. "If I didn't know better, I'd think you were worried."

"About what?" Delta demanded.

"Worried you might be tempted to come over here and molest me in the middle of the night."

She laughed airily. "You *wish.* If anybody has to be worried, it's me, considering you keep bringing up the possibility of us hooking up—which we won't."

"Six months is a long time," he said.

"According to you, you've gone without for months, so abstinence isn't a problem. But you know what? I don't believe you. I think *I* need to be concerned that you'll molest me in the middle of the night. Matter of fact..."

She sat up and placed two of her pillows end to end between them and plopped back down on the bed. Her head was lower, but she was too lazy to leave the bed to get more pillows from the hall closet.

Ignacio rolled onto his elbow and faced her. She tensed, eying him with distrust.

"Oh no, a wall of pillows!" he exclaimed in a mocking voice. "I'll never be able to get past this impenetrable fortress you created. Dammit." He shook his fist in mock anger and then dropped a heavy hand on one of the pillows.

The soft barrier seemed ridiculous now—a lame attempt to maintain distance when every nerve in her body was acutely aware of his presence. He could still make her... *feel* things.

Delta took a moment to glare at him and then rolled onto her side, tucking the duvet tightly under her arm. "You should have your agent try to get you more comedic roles. You're so funny—at least you think you are."

She lay on her side for a few minutes, but all she could think about was his tight body without a stitch of clothing in the bed with her. If she reached back, she would touch his—

She closed her eyes and fought the urge to push back against him, a move she used to make when she wanted to have sex. Then he'd place a hand on her hip and start kissing her neck, slowly sliding his hand higher until he cupped her breast and pinched her nipple between his fingertips. He would tease her until she was silently begging by grinding her ass against him, desperate for some part of him to be inside her—his finger, his tongue, his hard dick. Didn't matter, as far as she was concerned.

Delta drew a deep breath and moved restlessly. She pushed up on her elbow and punched the pillow, then plopped her head down again, releasing a frustrated breath.

"Are you okay over there?" Ignacio asked.

"I'm fine," she said grumpily.

"All your moving around is making it difficult for me to fall asleep."

"You could always go to one of the guest rooms," Delta said with saccharine sweetness.

Ignacio didn't respond. He didn't move, but she could sense him watching her. She *knew* he was. The back of her neck became warm, and her body slowly tightened under the weight of his stare.

Finally, after what seemed like forever, the mattress shifted as he rolled away.

"Good night, *mi amor*."

This was the first time he had used the endearment since she had shown up at his place in California. The mocking tone had been removed from the words, and his voice sounded warmer—almost like an invitation. As if he were trying to seduce her.

But that was her imagination... wasn't it? Ignacio was having a good time teasing and harassing her.

He didn't *really* want her... did he?

Chapter Fourteen

Reunited and It Feels So Good: Our Favorite Couple is Instagram Official

Another positive article about him and Delta, featuring the photo from his Instagram profile, which had garnered hundreds of thousands of likes and comments. Thanks to all the recent positive press, one of Delta's old singles had re-entered the top twenty yesterday, and the publicity was opening new doors. Offers were pouring in for them to promote everything from jewelry to luxury cars.

Ignacio placed his phone in his pocket and paced the foyer. He was in the process of straightening his cuffs when Delta started descending the stairs. He paused, his entire body going still and his mouth going dry as he watched her move with innate elegance, practically floating down each step.

Her team had done an amazing job with long extensions that brought her hair all the way down to her hips in bone straight strands parted in the middle. She wore a black and silver choker that matched her silver dress and held a Hermès clutch in her hand, a dark Loro Piana cashmere stole draped over one arm.

She was pure temptation in a sleeveless babydoll dress that stopped at the middle of her thighs, highlighting her show-stopping legs in a pair of sky-high heels. She looked very much like the superstar she was—glamorous, captivating, radiant. His eyes followed her all the way to the bottom step.

"I guess I don't have to ask you how I look," she said softly.

With her back straight and her full, perky breasts sitting high on her chest, she exuded confidence.

"I'm sure you know you look absolutely..." He never considered himself at a loss for words, yet here he was again, struggling to adequately describe the vision before him.

He walked over and trailed his fingers through the straight strands of her hair. The scent of her perfume filled his nostrils and wrapped around him like a silk ribbon, making his dick swell in his black trousers. The floral sweetness wasn't overpowering but would certainly linger in the air long after she had walked away.

"Stunning," he whispered.

"Thank you. You look pretty stunning yourself." Her sultry eyes flicked over his attire—a dark jacket, white shirt, and dark slacks.

She smoothed a hand over his chest, and the slow movement echoed inside him. It was just the two of them in the foyer. There was no one to perform for or to take pictures. And her touch—it didn't feel fake. It felt very, very real, very meaningful. When she lifted her gaze to his, he saw the unmistakable presence of heat in her eyes.

"We should go?" she suggested.

All of a sudden, he didn't want to go to the birthday party.

He had the urge to toss her over his shoulder and run upstairs so he could do every nasty thing he ached to with his tongue and hands.

"I guess we have to," Ignacio said roughly.

He helped her wrap the stole around her shoulders and then took her hand, threading his thicker fingers between her slender ones. Surprise filled her face because there was no one here to see them, but he ignored her expression and led the way out the front door to where a chauffeur-driven white limo waited for them in the driveway. As they strolled down the walkway, he felt like a man who had stumbled upon a rare and priceless treasure—one he couldn't let go.

After helping her into the vehicle, he slid onto the seat and watched from the corner of his eye as she crossed those impossibly smooth, sexy legs that had haunted his dreams all week. For the first five minutes of their ride, he sat stiffly in the seat, fighting the urge to gather her against him and kiss her tempting mouth until she was senseless. If he made it through the night without putting his fist through another man's face for looking at her, he deserved a damn prize.

Once he relaxed, he turned to Delta. "Which songs are you going to sing tonight?"

"King's assistant said his mother liked all my songs, but especially two slow songs from my second album: 'Beat of My Heart' and 'Love Me.' I'll sing those and include an up-tempo song in between."

"I like 'Love Me,'" Ignacio admitted.

Shock registered on her face, as if she couldn't believe he listened to her music.

"I know your music, and that song was one of the biggest on the album."

"It reached all the way to number three on the charts," she said, a soft smile on her lips.

"Should have been number one."

"I've had a couple of number ones," she said.

"The song you did with T-Murder went to number one, didn't it?"

Her biggest hit in recent years had been singing the hook on a Terrence "T-Murder" song for his last rap album before he retired, *Annihilation.* The video had accrued hundreds of millions of views, and at least one million of those views belonged to Ignacio. Over and over, he had watched one particular scene where Delta rolled around under the white satin sheets, her alluring body partially on display for the rapper.

"Our song did go to number one. He gave my career a boost, which helped since the last album didn't do well."

"It's all relative, though, isn't it? Like when people say one of my movies didn't do well because it made $200 million instead of $350 million domestically. There are actors who would kill for $200 million in domestic box office receipts."

"The corporations don't care. I think part of what fueled the success of the single with T-Murder was the buzz about the chemistry between us."

He remembered the chatter and had despised it. "*Did* something happen between you two?" He had no business asking but needed to know.

"Absolutely not," Delta said vehemently. "Terrence was back with his wife by then. Believe me, the man was not interested in me. Strictly work. He had a bad reputation, but that was in the past."

"I should be used to the lies. Apparently, I have a number of illegitimate children. My youngest love child is in Mexico, being cared for by one of my aunts."

Delta laughed. "I hadn't heard that."

"One day I'll have to tell you about my six or seven children around the world."

"I can't wait," she replied with a giggle.

Damn, it was good to talk to her again and hear her bubbly laugh.

Not long afterward, they arrived at the home of Benjamin Brockwell, King Brockwell's father, where the birthday party was taking place. They entered a room filled with a few dozen guests, and the people near the door gasped and whispered to each other when they saw the couple. King immediately appeared and greeted them.

"Delta J, it's nice to finally meet you," he said.

Ignacio's gaze lowered to where King held Delta's hand between both of his. Did he have to hold on to her that long?

"Nice to meet you too," she replied.

"Can I introduce you to my mother?"

"Please. She's the reason I'm here."

"Keep in mind, she had no idea you were coming."

They walked over to Elizabeth Brockwell, a brown-skinned woman with lively eyes. She was tall, almost six feet, which let Ignacio know the Brockwell brothers had inherited their height from both parents. Benjamin Brockwell stood beside his wife.

When she saw them, Elizabeth's eyes brightened even more, and her mouth fell open. "Delta J? Wh—"

"Happy birthday, Mother," King said, looking mighty pleased with himself.

Elizabeth pressed a hand to her chest. "I cannot believe you invited her here for me."

"He didn't just invite me. I'm singing, and if you think I'm here to sing happy birthday, think again."

"Oh my goodness."

Delta hooked her arm through Elizabeth's. "How about I sing two of your favorites, 'Beat of My Heart' and 'Love Me'?"

Elizabeth laughed. "This is incredible. I would be honored

for you to do that for me." She looked at her son and then her husband.

Benjamin smiled. "This was all King's doing. We wanted to make tonight special for you, and this was the best way we knew how."

"Well, it's certainly very special, and I can't wait to hear you sing." Tears brimmed in Elizabeth's eyes, and Ignacio couldn't imagine the strain her diagnosis had placed on her and her family.

"This is Ignacio Santana, Delta's partner," King said.

Elizabeth studied his face. "You look familiar. Do I know you?"

"He's an actor, Mother, and we're producing one of his films."

"Oh my goodness, please forgive me. Despite the family business, I don't watch a lot of movies, but I do recognize your face. A gorgeous face like yours is unforgettable."

They all had a good laugh. Minutes later, they met King's younger brothers, Chance and Romeo, and then mingled with the rest of the guests, including the trio of musicians who were going to perform with Delta.

There was plenty of food and a DJ was playing music, but no one was dancing. Eventually, a staff member wheeled out a huge cake, and they all sang "Happy Birthday" to Elizabeth while she stood with her hands clasped together, her expression a mix of emotion and appreciation.

An hour and a half passed while they mingled and ate with the other guests. Then Delta left Ignacio's side to join her bandmates.

She stepped onto the small, elevated stage where the DJ had previously been performing, and the crowd quieted in anticipation. The lights dimmed, and the mini-concert began. Behind her was a pianist, but he might as well have been invisible because Delta was the star, with the chandelier above casting golden light on her dark brown skin.

As she sang the words to 'Beat of My Heart,' crooning into the microphone, she locked eyes with Ignacio. Was this part of her act, or was she sending him a message?

He couldn't help but feel as if she were singing *to* him, as if those words of love and devotion were real and directed specifically at him. Others must have had the same thought because several people turned in his direction with knowing smiles on their faces.

Ignacio sipped his drink. Act or not, emotion burned through him as he watched Delta clutching the mic and singing her heart out. After the first two songs, the applause was thunderous in the small space.

Delta's gaze swept the audience. "This last song, 'Love Me,' is very special to me. I co-wrote it with a very good friend of mine. It's a song about love and longing. I know it's one of your favorites." She smiled at Elizabeth seated in front of the stage. "It's one of mine too."

When Delta began to sing, a hushed silence fell over the audience once again. The depth of emotion in her voice filled every corner of the room. Elizabeth swayed in her seat in front of the stage, cradled in her husband's arms. Her three sons stood behind them.

Ignacio had heard Delta sing plenty of times, but he never grew tired of her voice and the magical way the words vibrated on her vocal cords. This song, in particular, had such a haunting melody that he ended up holding his breath.

Her rich, velvety voice trembled with raw emotion, each lyric weighted with longing and vulnerability. The melody, accompanied by the keystrokes of the piano, soared and dipped. Briefly, she closed her eyes, lost in the deep meaning of the words.

I can't breathe when you're not near
Stay with me, baby, stay right here
Don't you see what we could be?
I need you, hold me, love me

No one moved or whispered a word to their neighbor. She had entranced the entire room with the soulful sound of her voice. When she reached the final lingering note, Delta stretched her fingers toward the chandelier and belted out a sound that rivaled an angel's voice. She held the note for what seemed like an eternity.

Ignacio's throat tightened with emotion.

When she had left him, he had died inside. But how could he fault her for going after her passion? She was a natural, born to do this.

Delta finished the song with a drop of her head, and the lights went out. When they flashed back on, she lifted her head and smiled, and the room erupted into applause. Anyone sitting immediately sprang to their feet.

Ignacio was convinced her performance had transformed every person in the room into adoring fans. Guests whispered to each other and exchanged looks of awe. She hadn't simply performed her song.

She had imprinted "Love Me" into their hearts.

Chapter Fifteen

"Romeo said you're about to leave." King approached Delta at the bar, his voice deep and low as he spoke.

"I'm afraid so. I'm waiting for Ignacio. He's giving acting advice to a couple of your guests." She nodded toward Ignacio and two men talking less than ten feet away.

King followed her line of sight and chuckled. "Could be worse. They could be fawning all over him and demanding his autograph, I guess."

"I believe that's already happened," Delta said with some amusement.

King groaned.

She didn't know much about the Brockwells, except that they were very powerful in the media and entertainment industry. King, the oldest, was tall and undeniably attractive with dark brown skin. Despite his friendliness, there was an arrogant air about him. She suspected he had seen and done more in life than most people had.

His discerning eyes missed nothing, and the slight curve of his lips suggested he was always a step ahead of any competitor and always in control.

"I really appreciate you making an exception to sing for my mother. She was completely surprised, which is what we wanted—and very, very happy." His eyes found his parents across the room. "I can't believe a year ago we thought we'd lose her, but she's a fighter."

His love for his mother was evident.

"It was an honor to be a part of her birthday celebration."

Delta's father hadn't approved of her singing at the party, especially not for free, but she had overridden his decision. Elizabeth's reaction and words of appreciation had made every minute spent arguing with her father worthwhile.

"I believe you have new fans now, don't you?" King asked.

She laughed lightly. "I do, which is a nice bonus."

After she finished her set, some of the guests had crowded around her, and she signed autographs. The experience reminded her of the early days when she worked small venues to build a fan base.

Performing in an arena or amphitheater was electrifying, as thousands of voices sang the lyrics to the songs right along with her. The pulse of the music vibrated across her skin, and the sheer magnitude of the crowd's energy washed over her like a tidal wave. Few experiences offered such an exhilarating rush.

But there was something to be said for the smaller locations, similar to tonight's intimate gathering. It felt more personal because she could look at every face and feel the heightened emotions in the room. With no distance between them, she had a front-row seat to see how her songs affected the audience. She might not return to doing private engagements, but she'd talk to her father about smaller venues.

"So, you and Ignacio are back together for good, is that correct?"

"Yes, we are."

"Lucky bastard," King murmured, his eyes drifting over her bare shoulders.

Unexpectedly, Ignacio slipped an arm around her waist and pulled her against his side. Where had he come from?

"King, I hope everything went well?" he asked.

"Better than expected, thanks. I look forward to doing business with you. As for you, Delta—"

"Your business with her ends tonight, doesn't it?" Ignacio asked pointedly, his gaze meeting King's head-on.

Oh shit. Delta laughed to soften the delivery of Ignacio's words. What was he thinking? Was he trying to sabotage the deal with his fake jealousy act?

She slipped an arm around his waist and gazed up at him with a sidelong glance. "That's right. I'm done here, and now the two of you have a movie to make. Right, hon?"

"Yes, we do," Ignacio said, keeping his eyes on King.

A smile touched King's lips, as if he had received the message loud and clear. "We sure do. I'll be in touch." After a brief nod, he walked away.

Delta waited until he was out of earshot before speaking. "What the heck were you thinking, saying something like that to him?"

"You think I don't know he was hitting on you? You're here with me. Don't forget what we're doing."

She kept a smile on her face in case anyone was watching them. "Of course I haven't forgotten, but maybe you should smile. We wouldn't want people to think we're arguing. We want them to think we can't keep our hands off each other. King was being friendly, that's all. Maybe bring it down a notch before you jeopardize your deal."

"Fuck him," Ignacio said. He took a deep breath and let it out.

He was acting as if he were really jealous. *Was* he jealous of King Brockwell?

"Ignacio—"

He forced a smile, which didn't quite look real. "If telling him to stay the hell away from my woman jeopardizes the deal, then so be it."

My woman. He sounded as if he meant those words.

"Let's get out of here," he muttered.

On the way to the door, they picked up her stole from one of the chairs, and she threw the fabric around her shoulders. Taking her hand, Ignacio led the way toward the exit, but they didn't have a clean getaway. Several of the guests stopped them as they wound their way through the room, and they paused to say goodbye to Elizabeth and Benjamin.

"Thank you for such a lovely birthday present," the older woman said.

"You're welcome," Delta returned, giving her a warm hug.

Outside, Ignacio called for the limo, holding Delta's hand the entire time. Finally, the car pulled up, but he didn't wait for the chauffeur to climb out and open the door. He opened it himself and practically shoved her onto the seat, as if he wanted to get her as far away from King Brockwell as possible.

They rode in silence before Delta spoke. "Tonight was nice."

Ignacio kept his gaze on the scenery outside and grunted, his feet tapping the floor of the vehicle.

"You're not upset about King, are you?" Delta asked, though a small part of her hoped he was.

She experienced a thrill at the thought that maybe—just maybe—his behavior was a manifestation of jealousy. It would mean his feelings for her hadn't completely died when she never showed up that day.

"What the hell kind of name is King?" he demanded. "A kid named King is bound to have a superiority complex."

"I think it's kind of a cool name," Delta murmured.

He shot her an angry look, and she lowered her gaze, turning away so he couldn't see her amusement.

He is jealous! Ohmigod, she thought. Her heart skipped and thrummed like a drumbeat, fast and unsteady, echoing through her chest.

When they pulled up to the house, Ignacio helped her out of the car.

"Thank you," she said.

His fingers tightened around hers as he tugged her toward the front door. He released his grip on her hand to punch in the door code, and she stepped in ahead of him.

The second the door closed, she felt his hand on her wrist. He spun her around and pressed her back against the cool foyer wall, his body flush against hers, his breath warm and irregular.

Delta gasped in shock. Her clutch slipped from her fingers and hit the floor. "What are you doing?" she whispered, her voice trembling.

The air crackled with anticipation, making her heart hammer in her throat. Framing her face in his hands, Ignacio tilted her chin higher.

"Losing my fucking mind," he grated.

He kissed her. Not gently. Not carefully. He claimed her with an urgency that left no room for doubt about his intentions.

Slanting his mouth over hers, he coaxed her lips apart, and she welcomed him, surrendering to the passionate heat coiling low in her abdomen. His hands slipped down her sides, gripping her hips to hold her in place while her fingers tangled in his thick curls and pulled him closer.

His tongue entered her mouth to stroke, tease, and deepen the intimate contact. The kiss became hotter and wetter as they devoured each other.

Then a quiet sound caught Delta's attention. She almost didn't hear it, but Ignacio must have heard it, too, because he tore his mouth from hers, and they both looked to the side in the same direction.

Maria was in her bathrobe holding a plate of food, frozen mid-stride like a cartoon character. She was obviously trying to tiptoe across the floor to the door leading to her apartment in the basement.

She looked at them. They looked at her.

"I am so sorry, Ignacio, Delta. Pretend you do not see me." Her cheeks were scarlet, and her face filled with apology. Then she hurried through the door and shut it behind her.

Ignacio stepped back, a muscle in his jaw tightening.

Delta didn't know what to say. She tried to catch her breath. She hadn't been kissed with such passion in a long time. She put a hand to her throbbing mouth. "I guess—"

"This isn't going to work," he said in a guttural tone. He shoved unsteady fingers through his hair and swore softly.

Delta died a little inside. "What isn't?"

"Living together and acting as if we don't feel anything. Lying in the same bed together. All I can think about is getting you naked and fucking you until we're both sweaty and exhausted. I know that wasn't part of the deal, but it's incredibly hard to keep my hands off you." The words came out in a mixture of disgust and anger.

"Sex will complicate this whole charade." She wasn't sure she meant the words, but they sounded right.

"It's already complicated."

The way he looked at her—as if he wanted to sweep her into his arms and carry her up the stairs—sent shivers racing down her spine.

Delta broke eye contact and moved to pick up her clutch and the few items that had fallen out of it. As she picked up her lipstick and phone, Ignacio reached down and closed his fingers around the smooth bluish-gray stone on the floor.

She straightened, holding her breath, cursing herself for not grabbing it before he saw. Ignacio stared at the stone in his palm, an unreadable expression on his face.

"You still have this?" His voice was low and disbelieving.

"It's stupid, I know." Fully embarrassed, Delta thrust out her hand to take it.

He didn't hand it over. "Why do you still have this?"

She swallowed, emotion burning a hole in her throat. "You gave it to me."

"It's just a stone."

"It's more than a stone. It's my good luck charm."

He had given her the stone when they were both fifteen, telling her it came from a river in Colombia near his mother's home. He said it stood out from the other jagged rocks and gravel around it, and because of that, he thought of her—strong and beautiful, standing out from the crowd. No matter how rough the waters of the music industry became, he believed she would always endure.

"I rub it before live performances," she admitted in a low voice. "And I carry it everywhere. In a way, I feel like it keeps me safe. The one time I didn't have it..." She couldn't finish.

"What happened?"

"Something bad." Unable to look at him, she extended her hand again.

"What happened, Delta?"

"Give it to me, Ignacio. Please." She lifted her gaze, her eyes turning watery.

"If someone hurt you—"

She snatched the rock and walked away. "Don't ask questions you don't want to hear the answer to," she said, and raced up the stairs.

Chapter Sixteen

Ignacio couldn't let it go.

He couldn't forget what Delta had said or the look on her face when she said *Something bad.*

A heaviness rested in his stomach—one he couldn't shake because he knew what had happened to her was worse than bad, more than likely terrible. The way she ran away from him proved it.

He took the box of cigarettes from the shelf in the kitchen cabinet and tapped one out.

No.

The stress of dealing with Delta and wanting to control his emotions was driving him to smoke again. Of course, if he really wanted to stop, he wouldn't have them in the house.

He shoved the cigarette back into the box and tossed the box on the shelf. He then took two stairs at a time to the second floor and pushed his way inside their bedroom. Delta was coming out of the bathroom and pulled up short.

"We need to talk," he said.

"There's nothing to talk about."

"You dropped a bombshell on me. You can't expect me to go to sleep and pretend our conversation didn't happen."

She sighed wearily, tucking some of her long hair behind her ear. "Why not?"

"Because I won't be able to rest until you tell me what you're keeping from me."

"We're not really in a relationship, so you don't have to pretend—"

"You think I'm pretending to be concerned? I'm not fucking pretending, Delta!" He dragged a hand down his face, fighting to harness his emotions. *This damn woman.* "You want to know something embarrassing? For the past eleven years, I've stalked your social media. In my head, I've punched my fist through the face of every man you've walked the red carpet with or smiled at in a photo. This isn't fake! I wanted to forget about you—us—everything we meant to each other and I can't. My heart won't let me. I can't fit anyone else in here"—his fist hit his chest—"because you take up all the goddamn space!"

He hadn't expected such passionate words to spill from his mouth, and clearly neither had Delta. She stared at him in shock, temporarily speechless. "I—I didn't know you felt that way," she said quietly.

"You weren't supposed to." He spoke in a low, tired tone, but a weight had been lifted from his shoulders. "I can't deny the truth anymore. Losing you—destroyed me."

Her lips parted as tears sprang to her eyes. "I didn't mean to hurt you."

"Why did you send your father to see me? We were supposed to get married. I had a ring, I—" He broke off in frustration.

"I know. I know, but I had responsibilities. My family was depending on me, and you—you were blowing up. I was blowing up, too, and I had so much work to do."

"We were supposed to grow together and share in each other's success. That's what we discussed."

"I know, I remember." She swallowed. "But it's not as if you hung around for very long."

"What are you talking about?"

"Right after you and my father talked, I reached out to you, and you were gone. You left the country and wouldn't return my phone calls."

"You sent your father to break up with me," he reminded her in a hard voice.

"I didn't *send* him," she denied. "My parents thought it was best if he talked to you, but I regretted letting him go in my place, and then you were gone. The next time I saw you was in pictures with that Mexican actress. You didn't even fight for us."

"So you wanted me to grovel, is that it?" Ignacio demanded.

"I wanted you to fight for us, despite what happened."

He clenched his jaw. "Do you have any idea what it was like to wait for you at the airport and have your father show up instead? To tell me you weren't coming? To tell me to leave you alone once and for all, like I never meant anything to you? The whole time I had a ring in my pocket because we agreed to get married."

"I was scared," she whispered.

"And I was hurt. Destroyed. *Destroyed*," he repeated, leaning toward her, his voice strained.

"You got engaged to Lori Stanfield less than three months after we broke up!" Delta yelled.

"It didn't mean anything!"

"Pictures of the two of you were all over the entertainment news, and you gave her a huge diamond," she said, jabbing her finger at his face.

"I wanted to hurt you," Ignacio admitted. "I wanted you to

see what you were missing, and I wanted to prove to you and the world that I was fine without you."

"Well, you did an excellent job." Delta folded her arms over her chest. "I was crushed," she whispered.

Ignacio laughed bitterly. "I guess we both were."

"I know you don't believe me, but I loved you," Delta said.

"Loved me? You had a funny way of showing it. I lost track of how many times you broke up with me." Ignacio tossed his jacket on a chair and paced the room restlessly, trying to calm his chaotic thoughts.

Yanking open the curtains, he stared out at the dark night, barely seeing the expansive yard and the covered swimming pool.

"I never wanted to," she said in a low voice.

Ignacio let out a short laugh and stuffed a hand in his pants pocket. "Right."

Silence took over the room for a long time, as if neither of them was willing to speak and break the temporary peace. Then he heard her voice, quiet and trembling.

"I was assaulted when I was sixteen."

He spun to face her. She had spoken so softly, he was hoping he'd heard wrong. "What did you say?"

Delta pulled air into her lungs and met his gaze. "I was assaulted at sixteen," she said again. "By someone who worked for the record company."

Ignacio couldn't move. He became rigid, his body locking in place. "Sixteen? That's when we..."

She nodded. "It happened not long after you and I lost our virginity to each other."

A mix of terror and anger thundered through him. "Who?"

She shook her head. "I don't want to say."

Seconds dragged by, and he remained silent, allowing her the opportunity to speak again when she was ready.

"My parents put too much trust in him. They left me with him over the weekend—"

"Over the weekend? *The fucking weekend?*"

She continued speaking in a low, monotonous voice. "He said he wanted to develop my talent and suggested intensive training. There were supposed to be two other girls working with me, but they never showed up. I don't know if they were really supposed to be there or if he made the whole thing up. He and I were the only ones at his house over the weekend. At first, everything was fine, and we practiced my dances, and he helped me vocally. That was Friday night. I realize now he was getting me to trust him. On Saturday... I was in my room, and he came in..."

Her voice quivered, and he recognized how difficult it was for her to continue.

"How did I not know this?" Ignacio whispered.

"You were in Panama working on a project with your father. I couldn't reach you, and the opportunity came up to work closely with him, so we took it. When you came back, I broke up with you."

"I remember," he said slowly. "I thought you were upset because I had been gone for a long time."

It was the first breakup in their on-and-off relationship over the years. He hadn't understood why she dumped him and had experienced mixed emotions for a long time afterward. On one hand, he had been flattered because he assumed she had become upset about their time apart. On the other hand, he couldn't believe she thought that was a valid reason to end their relationship. The whole time, she had been silently suffering. His insides tightened with sorrow.

"I had this weird mixture of guilt and shame—like I'd cheated on you. I felt dirty and... and not good enough for you. I was so confused."

"I had no idea."

"You weren't supposed to."

"How many people know what happened to you?"

"Not many. You're the second person I've told. The first was my therapist."

Her response temporarily stunned him into silence.

"What about your parents?"

She shook her head.

"Delta, you should tell them."

"No."

"It's clear what happened still bothers you. Maybe if you opened up and told—"

"I went to therapy and learned to deal with what happened. The truth is, I got what I wanted. I received a record deal, and everybody called me the next hottest thing in R&B. So what if some days I feel like a fraud, like I'm going to wake up one morning and the world will know how I achieved my success? So what if I'm hiding this horrible secret and don't know if I was really good because of how I got the contract?"

Her flippant tone betrayed her pain.

Ignacio walked to her and gripped her shoulders. "*You are good,*" he said fiercely. "You're an amazing, talented, beautiful person. You sing, dance, and write. You move people with your music. Your performance tonight was incredible, and it's always like that."

She smiled wanly.

"I'm not just saying that, Delta. You're a rare talent."

"Thank you."

Looking into her eyes, he saw the young woman he'd been obsessed with since he was a teenager. If he could go back in time, he would protect her from that pain.

"I loved you so much."

A faint smile softened her lips. "I wanted to marry you,

Ignacio, but I wasn't sure. I was scared, and I had this horrible secret. And we were *young*. Only twenty-one years old. But I loved you too, and I didn't want to lose you. I wish I'd made a different decision eleven years ago."

"Me too. I should have come to find you. I gave up too easily," he said.

"We both did."

He wasn't sure who moved first. It could have been him. It could have been her.

All he knew was that one minute they were gazing into each other's eyes, and the next their mouths were sealed together in a heartrending kiss.

Chapter Seventeen

Ignacio kissed Delta so passionately it was as if he had been waiting forever to place his stamp on her again. It felt good to touch him and be touched by him.

She moaned and pressed her aching nipples against his hard chest, sliding her fingers into his silky hair and crushing her mouth against his. His tongue roamed the inside of her mouth, and she moaned, grinding her hips against his hard dick poking her in the belly.

They quickly undressed, tearing off each other's clothes with urgent hands, their progress hindered by the relentless press of kisses against every newly exposed inch of skin. By the time they made their way to the bed, she was feverish with need and slightly breathless.

Hovering over her, his masculine gaze darkened with appreciation. She pulled him down on top of her, desperate for more, aching for his mouth and hands to cover every inch of her body. He dropped hot kisses down her throat, along her collarbone, to the swell of her breasts, and her nipples hardened and quivered with anticipation.

"God, I've missed you," he whispered huskily.

"Not nearly as much as I've missed you," she whispered back.

His hands were on her breasts, stroking the nipples with the edges of his thumb. She loved the way he touched her—possessive yet tender, focused on making sure she received the utmost pleasure. Biting her lip, she relished the sweet, sweet torture. Then he tugged the tight peak of her left breast into his mouth, and all she could do was gasp aloud.

The pleasure was immediate and intense. How long had it been since she'd had his mouth on her like this? *Years*. Much too long.

She knotted her fingers in his soft curls as his tongue played with the pebbled flesh. He felt so good. He made her ache. Quietly, she begged him to do the same to the other breast.

He willingly obliged, alternating between them, showering each one in turn with lingering kisses and strokes of his tongue while his hand caressed her open thighs—exploring her wet sex as he primed her for his possession.

And she wanted it. She longed to feel him inside her, to take her hard and bring her to the brink of insanity.

Ignacio kissed the underside of her breasts and then went lower with heated, open-mouth kisses. His tongue played with her navel. He sucked the soft flesh of her abdomen. Then he spread her legs to the width of his broad shoulders.

"Nacio," she panted, barely able to speak.

He had complete control of her, and she was dizzy with desire.

Then his head was between her thighs, and his probing tongue was at her slick entrance. Her cries grew louder, her head angling backward on the pillow. He knew exactly how to please her. He teased and prodded, licking and sucking, driving her out of her mind. Her hips bucked against his mouth as he continued to indulge, taking his fill while moaning his satisfaction.

The sounds of him eating her were unbearably erotic. She twisted in agony, fighting to prolong the pleasure, but she orgasmed hard, fingernails sinking into the sinewy muscles of his wide shoulders. Her strangled cries bounced off the walls as his relentless mouth dragged her over the cliff into the greatest pleasure she had ever known. It had been so long since she'd felt this way, and he made her feel like no other man could.

Her first love. Her first lover. No one else could compare.

"*Deliciosa.* You taste just as delicious as I remember. Better, even," he rasped.

Their mouths fused together in another passionate kiss. His long fingers continued to roam her body, caressing her inner thighs, stroking the curve of her hips, squeezing the softness of her breasts. In return, she ran her hands over his beautiful body, her fingers pressing into his swarthy skin and firm muscles as he rocked against her, the length of his hard dick pressed to her core.

Slowly, he rolled onto his back, and it was her turn to make love to him. She licked his chest and teased his flat brown nipples with her tongue. She listened to his breath hitch as she ran her hands over the firm muscles of his abdomen and watched as they bunched in response to her touch.

"I need you. Now," Ignacio said huskily.

His eyes were the darkest she had ever seen, and his face had transformed into harsh lines of lust.

He pushed her onto her back and stretched her hands above her head. Pushing her thighs apart with his knee, he used one hand to lift one of her legs and pushed himself inside her. Her mouth fell open, and a low wail escaped. He was inside her again. *Finally.* Tears sprang to her eyes as he sank deeper and filled her body with his hard length.

They rocked back and forth on the mattress, her breasts jiggling, and each stroke making her gasp, echoing the sound of his throaty groans.

"Delta, Delta, Delta."

She lifted her knees toward her chest, and he sank even deeper. Closing her eyes, she concentrated on the delicious sensation of him sliding in and out of her drenched sex.

"Nacio," she whispered. His name on her lips was little more than a pained, breathless plea.

"I could die in this pussy. I could fucking die," Ignacio panted. His breath hit the side of her neck as he rammed harder in the race toward mutual satisfaction.

The tightness in her belly suddenly loosened, and shudders racked her body. Her mouth fell open on a silent cry of ecstasy.

He felt so damn good. She couldn't stop shaking. She couldn't stop moaning.

He was absolutely right. He *had* gotten better.

In the middle of the night, Delta woke up when Ignacio pressed his lips to the exact spot where his initial was located on her right shoulder blade. The room was dark, and his body was wrapped around her from behind, one hair-roughened leg nestled between her smooth thighs.

"Why didn't you remove it?" Ignacio asked in a soft voice.

Lying about the significance of the tattoo was easy, but remove it? Impossible. She could have even had a tattoo artist place another design over the initial, yet she hadn't.

"Why didn't you remove yours?" she asked.

He didn't answer the question either.

He smoothed a hand down her back and over the curve of her backside, and right away arousal throbbed to life between her thighs. Making love one time wasn't enough for him, and it wasn't enough for her. They had so much time to make up for.

He brushed her hair away from her neck and kissed the exposed skin while his hand slipped to the front and covered her right breast. She pushed back against him and rubbed her butt against his burgeoning erection. Ignacio rolled her onto her stomach and pushed her thighs apart. Burying her face in the pillows, Delta let out a soft mewl as he entered her from behind. Her fingers tightened in the bedsheets, and she arched her ass higher.

The speed and power of his thrusts gradually increased.

"Nacio, Nacio," she panted in the darkness.

Cuffing the back of her neck, he drove into her with longer, harder strokes. She kept his rhythm, her body instinctively moving with his in perfect sync.

Splaying her hands against the headboard, Delta bit down on her lip until the tightening in her lower abdomen forced her to close her eyes.

"Nacio..." Her voice cracked on his name, and she shuddered as orgasmic waves overtook her body.

He muttered a stream of Spanish curses as his body, too, trembled under the force of his climax. Burying his face in the side of her neck, he slammed a hand against the headboard as the last bit of tremors quivered through his body. With a grunt signaling his energy had been depleted, he collapsed against her back, crushing her into the mattress.

Later, as Delta dozed off with Ignacio's body wrapped around hers again, she had two distinct thoughts: being with other men had never felt this good, and after tonight, everything would change.

Chapter Eighteen

Eyes closed while gripping her headphones, Delta belted out the end of "Sexy Lover" into the microphone. When she stopped, she opened her eyes and looked at the two men seated behind the glass—super producer Lance Row and engineer Taz.

She waited, already anticipating Lance's words. *That wasn't good enough.* She had been in the studio since this morning and was having an off day.

Lance, tall with chocolate skin and a voice suggesting he had missed his own calling as an R&B crooner, leaned into the microphone. "Good, but not good enough, sweetheart. You can do better, and you were a little pitchy at the end. Do you need a break?"

Resting her hands on her hips, Delta shook her head. "No, let's try it again." She took a sip of water and cleared her throat.

The average person wouldn't notice the difference in each performance, but she was a perfectionist, which was why she liked working with Lance. He didn't tolerate mediocrity and pushed her to improve.

"From the top," he said.

Delta nodded and stepped closer to the microphone to sing the words written for her by one of the top writers contracted by the record company. In the dimly lit booth, she gripped the headphones as she immersed herself in the song. The memorized lyrics flowed easily from her lips, while on the other side of the glass, Taz and Lance listened intently and nodded in time to the beat.

Near the end of verse one, she saw the door to the control room open from the corner of her eye and knew before looking that Ignacio had arrived. She had been expecting him. He had come to the studio yesterday as well. Her attention shifted to him as he greeted the producer and engineer. Then his gray eyes focused on her, and suddenly the words of the song took on a new meaning.

She kept her eyes on him as he stood behind the other men with his broad shoulders and an unreadable expression on his face. Swaying in time to the rhythm, her fingers flexed as she reached for an invisible person just beyond her grasp, her voice rising and falling as she expressed desire for her secret lover.

Heat coiled in her stomach. The sexy words weren't simply words. They were a testimony.

Sexy lover, you set my body on fire
Every kiss, every touch takes me higher
Love me hard, love me fast, love me slow
Don't walk away, please don't let me go

I love looking at you, you're so fine
Every touch sends chills down my spine
I'm in heaven when we're all alone
And you whisper my name in that dark, sexy tone
That dark, that dark, sexy tone

At the end of the song, she was gripping the microphone and singing with a sultrier edge and emotional depth in her voice.

"Yes!" Lance's hand shot in the air with blatant approval. "That's what I'm talking about."

Taz slow-clapped. "Nailed it," he said.

"I guess that was better?" Delta asked with a laugh, removing the headphones.

"I love how you gradually increased the intensity, and when you held the note at the end..." Lance kissed his fingertips.

"Sounds like we have what we need. Break time?"

"You're allowed," Lance said with a grin. He checked his watch. "Let's meet back here at three-thirty?"

"Sounds good to me." Delta exited the booth and watched Lance and Taz leave through the outer door.

"Hey," she said softly.

"Hey." Ignacio pulled her into his arms, and she melted against the firmness of his chest, enjoying the way his mouth moved over hers in a slow, languid kiss.

One would think her appetite would be assuaged after they'd had sex multiple times in the past couple of weeks, but the opposite had happened. She craved him a hundred times more, and they couldn't keep their hands off each other, as if making up for all the years they had been apart.

"Mmm," Delta said as she withdrew. Picking up her purse from the leather sofa, she asked, "What did you think of my performance?"

"I'm sure you know you did an excellent job. What's the name of the song?" Ignacio guided her through the door with a hand at the base of her spine.

"Sexy Lover."

"One of yours?"

"No, the record company gave it to me." Delta slipped a pair of oversized designer sunglasses over her eyes. "Where are we going to eat?"

"A little Korean spot a couple of miles away. Randall and Ava are meeting us there."

"Is it the dumpy-looking place?"

"That's the one," Ignacio confirmed.

"The food is so good there."

They climbed into Ignacio's Corvette, and he gunned the engine. Last night he told her his mother had invited her to Thanksgiving dinner. He expected an answer today, but she hadn't yet decided what to do. Thankfully, he hadn't brought up the invitation again.

Before pulling away, he spoke in a low tone to her. "Don't be obvious, but do you see what I see across the street, at the brown brick building with the *For Lease* sign?"

Delta turned her head ever so slightly. A figure lurked in the bushes in front of the building, their form obscured but not their presence. The trembling leaves gave them away, as did the unmistakable glint of sunlight bouncing off a camera lens.

"I see them," she murmured, her voice steady despite the sudden awareness prickling her skin. She hoped the photos were flattering. She had her hair secured in a ponytail and had kept her makeup minimal.

"The pictures will work in our favor. Keep the conversation alive about us."

Delta nodded. "True," she said, though she didn't know how to feel about their situation anymore. They were having sex, kissing, and touching like a normal couple, and Ignacio expressed concern for her as a caring lover would.

A couple of days ago, she caught him staring at her, and when their eyes met, he simply smiled. Later that evening, he tried to convince her to tell him who had hurt her at sixteen, but she refused. She would never tell.

She wanted to forget the worst day of her life. She had done a lot of work to move past the trauma, but she was also afraid—of what Ignacio would do.

She cast a sidelong glance at him.

If he went after this man, there could be repercussions for her and her family right when her career was picking up again. There could be repercussions for Ignacio too. The executive was powerful and his influence far-reaching. He had much more power and influence than when he had abused her, and he could jeopardize Ignacio's deal with Brockwell Media and harm his career in other ways.

After a short drive, they arrived at the restaurant, and Randall and Ava stepped out of their respective vehicles. Randall led the way inside, with Ava following behind Delta and Ignacio.

They entered the small restaurant with its dingy glass windows and a handwritten sign near the door announcing the day's specials. The low hum of conversation mixed with the sizzle from the open kitchen, where a cook flipped slices of beef on the grill, and from which the scent of savory spices floated through the air. A narrow counter ran along one wall, lined with jars of homemade kimchi and pickled radishes.

A young waitress greeted them with a nod as she stacked bowls onto a tray. Then she paused and stared at them for a moment. Delta recognized the expression. She was starstruck—shocked to see them enter the establishment.

The waitress snapped out of her trance and told them to take any free booth. Most of them had cracked vinyl seats, some patched with duct tape. Delta and Ignacio found a table near the back and sat across from each other, with their bodyguards taking a table nearby. Delta took a moment to peruse the laminated menu she pulled from a rack on the table.

Despite the humble surroundings, the food was as delicious as dishes in any Michelin-starred restaurant. When she had visited in the past, she had waited in the car while an assistant or one of her bodyguards came inside to pick up the order she had placed over the phone. The restaurant wasn't very crowded at the moment because it was after two o'clock, but around lunchtime, every table would be occupied, and one time she had seen a line out the door.

After a few minutes, the same waitress came and took their order. To her credit, she left them alone without mentioning that she recognized either of them.

"So, are you going to keep me in suspense? How did the meeting with King Brockwell go today?" Delta asked.

Ignacio's team and the Brockwell team had been negotiating over the past couple of weeks. He had gone to their offices today to sign the contracts and take promotional photos.

"All done. We signed the contracts."

Delta gasped and let out a little squeal. Ignacio laughed at her reaction.

"So it's a done deal?" she asked.

"It's a done deal."

"Oh my goodness!" She covered his hands with hers. "Congratulations, baby."

As soon as the endearment left her mouth, she realized how it sounded—intimate, familiar, something a girlfriend would say.

Her cheeks warmed, and she immediately wished she could take back her outburst. She tried to pull her hands back, but he grabbed them, holding her in place. His light eyes searched hers, and she inhaled, holding her breath, wondering what he would say.

"Thank you."

Phase one of their agreement was complete. He had officially secured funding. Next, she had to finish her album and release a single. "When do you expect to start filming?"

"King has a writer in mind to look at the script and make revisions. Once we're in pre-production, there's a lot of work to do—assembling the rest of the cast, scouting locations, and working on the shooting schedule. I don't expect us to start production until next year, after I'm finished with my next film."

"But you should have the movie shot, edited, and released in time for awards season, like he wants?" Delta asked.

"I don't see why not. With an indie film, we won't have the same restrictions as a big production."

The waitress arrived with their drinks, and Ignacio released Delta's hands. Feeling bereft, she sipped her soda, fighting the urge to reach for him again.

"How do you feel about the album?"

"Good and bad—mostly good. I still haven't decided on a name yet, but I'm tossing around a few ideas. I also have a couple of songs I want to include that I wrote. I talked to Dad about it, but..." She shook her head.

"No go?"

"He thinks I should listen to A&R and stick to the sexy songs. Sex sells, et cetera, et cetera." She tapped a manicured nail on the tabletop in irritation. "The songs I want to include are love songs. 'Bad Behavior' is about a woman who's crazy in love and the bad decisions she makes because of her feelings. 'Unworthy' is...well, I'm sure you can figure out what it's about. The lyrics are sad and nostalgic, and I know their meaning will touch listeners."

"You're giving up?"

"I considered giving up, but then I asked myself, what

would Ignacio do?" She rested her chin on her hand. "So no, I'm not giving up. I'll finish the album with the songs they want me to, but I'm going to work with Lance to record *my* songs that I'll share with A&R when I go to New York next month. I really believe once they hear them, they'll change their minds. At least I hope so." She crossed her fingers.

The food arrived, and they ate their meals, both of them cleaning their plates. On the way out, the manager asked if he could take a photo of them. The request turned into them taking pictures with him, members of the staff, and other patrons. They signed autographs and then headed back to the studio.

When Ignacio parked, he turned to her. "Have you decided about Thanksgiving?"

"I was hoping I could avoid giving you an answer," Delta said, using a joking tone, though she wasn't joking.

Ignacio knew it, too, because he didn't laugh. "My brothers know the truth, but everyone else in my family believes our relationship is real."

His parents wanting to see her made sense. She hadn't visited them since she and Ignacio "reconciled," but she wasn't sure spending Thanksgiving with the Connor-Santanas was a good idea. Granted, she and Ignacio were in a better place than at the beginning of this ruse, but they were supposed to be a temporary couple.

"Yes, I'll come to Thanksgiving dinner." She might as well get it out of the way.

"They won't give you a hard time. I promise." Ignacio squeezed her hand.

"I better get back to work," Delta said.

She hopped out of the car and went inside, wondering how she would get through Thanksgiving dinner with his family.

Chapter Nineteen

With nerves fluttering in her belly, Delta walked up the stairs and through the double doors of the home where Ignacio's family waited. She had visited this house numerous times when she was younger—first as a friend and later as a girlfriend. His father, Benicio, had built this mansion for their blended family decades ago. On part of the expansive grounds, Ignacio's stepmother had created a fruit and vegetable garden, which she tended to keep herself busy.

Delta knew Ignacio's family hadn't approved of their on-again, off-again relationship years ago. His sisters, especially, had seemed ready to claw her eyes out for hurting their brother. The rest of the family had been better at hiding their animosity, but Ignacio had hinted at their displeasure without explicitly saying they weren't happy. That's why she had taken great care with her appearance, hoping to impress his family and not reveal that their whole relationship had begun as a lie to the public.

She'd had her hair styled in body waves and wore dark

slacks with a cream-colored blouse. Ignacio looked handsome in a black button-down shirt and black slacks, his curly hair hanging loose on his shoulders.

After a member of the staff took their coats at the door, they walked through one of the arches toward the great room. As soon as they entered, everyone halted their conversations and stared at them.

Rose Santana, the matriarch of the family, was the first to rise from her chair and approach. "Well, hello. Welcome. It's good to see you again, Delta. I'm so glad you could join us for dinner. It's been a long time." She gave her a warm hug.

Delta melted into the petite woman's arms. "Thank you, Mrs. Santana."

Ignacio and Delta sat next to each other, and after brief welcomes from the rest of the family, the conversations resumed. She remembered that Ignacio had a big family, but it had gone through changes over the years.

Thiago was in the process of taking over his father's company. His sister Audra was now married with five children, Monica was engaged, Ethan had remarried, and Bruno was also married. Maxwell, the youngest, was on his way to becoming a doctor and had come home from his residency for the holiday, bringing friends with him. Ignacio's parents were no longer together, but according to him, they got along well, so she wasn't surprised to see his father at the house.

Finally, Rose stood. "There are so many of us today—too many to eat in the dining room, so dinner will be served in the party room, where we have tables set up."

After her announcement, she led the way out of the room.

"The party room?" Delta whispered.

"The huge sunroom at the back of the house," Ignacio explained.

"Oh, the one where part of the ceiling and most of the walls are made of glass?"

Ignacio nodded. "We started calling it the party room because that's where my parents hosted big gatherings for a while."

The room had been transformed to look like the ballroom of a hotel, with several tables covered in white tablecloths to accommodate the entire family. Along the main wall were more tables filled with covered dishes. Delta could already smell the food, and her stomach growled as she anticipated digging in.

"You all know Rosa likes to have the whole family together, so of course she's very happy right now," Benicio said.

The rest of the family laughed, while his ex-wife pursed her lips and shot him a playful glare. Her name was Rose, but Delta remembered he always called her Rosa.

"Do you like to have the whole family together too?" The question came from Junior, Audra's oldest child.

Benicio smiled indulgently at his grandson. "I do. I love these moments when we're all together. Our family is big and growing every year. Soon, I'll have another son." He turned his attention to Monica's fiancé, Andre. "And I have two more daughters now," he said, his gaze encompassing Skye and Marissa, his sons' wives. "Before we say grace, Ethan said he wanted to say a few words."

"Thank you." The oldest son acknowledged his father with a nod.

"He must be about to announce a very lucrative deal. The only time I've seen him look so pleased was when he secured funding for his mixed-use community," Ignacio murmured from the side of his mouth.

Delta only remembered meeting Ethan a handful of times in the past, but she recalled him being rather stoic. Horizon, his mixed-use community, was well-known in the Atlanta area.

"This announcement isn't mine alone." He took the hand of his wife, who was standing beside him in a loose-fitting, long-sleeved dress. "We wanted to share our good news with all of you. Skye and I are going to be parents."

A gasp went through the room, and the entire family erupted in cheers. Delta and the other guests joined in the congratulations, sharing pats on the back and hugs as everyone celebrated the excitement.

"That's why you're wearing that loose-fitting dress," Monica accused, pointing, which caused the Connor-Santana clan to burst into laughter.

Skye, grinning from ear to ear, placed a hand on her belly and showed off her bump.

Finally, everyone settled down, and Benicio clasped his hands together. Looking around the room, he said, "That was some unexpected but excellent news."

Bruno, the second oldest son, cleared his throat. "I have an announcement too, but it's hard to beat that."

Scattered laughter filled the room, followed by hushed silence.

"Since we cannot beat you, I guess we'll join you. Marissa and I are also pregnant."

Delta's mouth fell open as excited screams filled the room, followed by hugs and pats on the back as everyone congratulated them too. Once again, she offered her congratulations with the rest of the family and guests.

Rose's eyes filled with tears. "Is this really happening? Two babies at the same time? Oh, my goodness!"

"You're going to be busy, Mommy," Monica said, squeezing her mother into a one-armed hug.

"I'm ready," Rose said with confidence.

They all laughed.

When the room was quiet again, Benicio looked around at

his family. "Does anyone else have a pregnancy announcement before we say grace?" He waited, his eyes twinkling with humor as he surveyed the room of smiling faces. "All right, let us hold hands and bow our heads."

Benicio said a prayer to bless the food and for his sons and daughters-in-law and their unborn babies. Afterward, they all lined up to fill their plates. In addition to turkey, there was ham and various sides. Delta had already cheated once on her diet this past week, but she couldn't resist adding a helping of macaroni and cheese to her plate. She then perused the dessert table, and her mouth fell open. She turned to look at Ignacio, who was across the room talking to his brother Thiago.

She caught his eye and mouthed, *Chocolate chip cookies with macadamia nuts.*

He smiled, and that's when she realized he had put in a request to his mother. He was so thoughtful. The small gesture meant the world to her because he had paid attention and wanted her to have the treat.

"Are you going to stick around this time?" The surprising question came from Monica, Ignacio's sister, tall and slender with a short natural hairstyle. She held a plate of food in her hand as she waited for a reply.

"What do you mean?" Delta asked, playing dumb.

Monica eyed her with barely concealed annoyance, and Delta straightened her spine, refusing to be intimidated.

Monica leaned closer, as if about to share a secret. "Don't play games with my brother's emotions. Ignacio doesn't deserve that. If you care about him, act like it." A taut smile briefly lifted the corners of her mouth, and then she sauntered off to her table.

Great. As she'd suspected, not everyone was pleased she and Ignacio were supposedly back together. Being viewed as the bad guy in the relationship sucked.

As Delta made her way to her chair, Marissa and Skye sat next to each other at another table and immediately put their heads together. She felt a twinge of envy. They were about to become mothers, and she didn't know when or if she would ever have children. Could she strike the right balance between being a performer and a good mother? Plenty of women had done so before her, but she was well aware that having a supportive partner played an important role in ensuring balance and raising well-rounded children.

She cast a quick glance at Ignacio, who was filling his plate with food. Did he want children? They hadn't discussed the topic in any detail when they were younger, but they were both in their thirties now, and she didn't know what he wanted. She also didn't know if their "relationship" would last past the originally discussed six-month expiration date.

A wave of sadness overcame her, and she picked up her iced tea and took a huge swallow, wishing she had something much stronger. As she placed the glass on the table, a young girl with goddess braids approached with stars in her eyes.

"Hi," she said nervously.

"Hi." Delta smiled at her.

Ignacio arrived at that moment and placed his plate on the table. "This is my niece, Kerilyn. The last time you saw her, she was around five or six years old. She probably wants to know if she can have an autograph."

"Uncle Ignacio." The teenager's cheeks reddened.

"Am I wrong?"

She bit her lip and shook her head.

Ignacio slung his arm around his niece's shoulders. "She won't bite, I promise," he said.

"He's right, I don't," Delta said. "If you have something to write on, I'd be happy to give you my autograph."

The girl's face brightened. "Thank you. Oh my gosh, I'm

sorry for being such a dork, but I can't believe I'm eating Thanksgiving dinner with Delta J."

She handed over a piece of paper and a pen with a trembling hand.

"How do you spell your name?" Delta asked.

"How do I spell my name?" For a second, she appeared confused. As Ignacio opened his mouth to help her, she shook her head. "Oh my gosh, what am I doing? I know how to spell my name." She let out an embarrassed laugh. "K-E-R-I-L-Y-N."

Delta wrote a message and signed her name below it.

Kerilyn gazed at the message and then clutched the paper to her chest. "Thank you *so* much. Can I give you a hug?"

"You sure can." Delta stood and embraced her.

"Okay, I'll leave you alone now." Kerilyn rushed off to sit at the table with her mother.

Ignacio sat next to Delta. "Thanks for doing that."

"Of course. That's what we do."

"Looks like she's texting her friends now," he added.

Sure enough, his niece's thumbs were flying across her phone.

"What did Monica say to you a few minutes ago?"

Delta opened her mouth to answer honestly but thought better of it. No point in creating friction between the siblings. "She told me to get some ham—said it's pretty good. I'll get some when I go for seconds. I have plenty of room in my belly since I didn't eat much at home."

Her family had eaten their Thanksgiving meal earlier, but she had only had a small portion to save room for tonight's meal.

Ignacio sat back and watched her with a thoughtful expression. "Ham, huh?"

"Mhmm." She touched his thigh under the table. "Thank you for inviting me."

The distraction seemed to work. He covered her hand and squeezed. "I'm glad you came."

Delta picked up her fork. "You know I'm leaving with a bunch of those cookies, right?"

"I already know." Ignacio dropped his voice. "I asked Mama Rosa to set aside a container for you. It's in the kitchen."

Delta stared at him in disbelief. How had she let him go before?

He was perfect.

Chapter Twenty

Benicio chuckled heartily at the hilarious story he had just told his ex-wife, Rose. The punchline had landed perfectly.

There was a time when he thought he would never lie in this bed again, yet here he was, naked beneath the sheets. Rose wore a blue silk robe, and he reclined against her soft breasts, her arms wrapped around him from behind as they both laughed.

"You made that up," she said, her voice thick with amusement.

"It's a true story. I swear," Benicio insisted.

Ever since he had inserted himself on her vacation to the Greek Isles, their relationship had blossomed in the right direction. They'd already had a good relationship, but Rose had become friendlier and different in other ways—though he couldn't quite articulate how. He simply knew her well enough to realize she wasn't the same after the trip.

Perhaps it was in the way her gaze lingered on him or the way she made eye contact. Nothing overt, but definitely different. Using those cues, Benicio had pushed the envelope with more than platonic touches and flirtatious conversation, careful to keep his behavior away from the prying eyes of their children as much as possible.

Then, the night of their eldest son's wedding, she had invited him upstairs. That was the first night in years they had spent in each other's arms, making love and reconnecting in the most intimate way. By mutual agreement, they kept their liaisons a secret from their children—at least for the time being. His good friend, Oscar, thought he was loco, but Benicio didn't care. He had gotten his Rosa back.

So what if the kids and the general public didn't know? He didn't mind. In fact, he worried that if they shared their secret with family too soon, someone might tell Rose she was making a mistake. Or she might begin to doubt she had made the right decision. No, this was better, and it added excitement to their meetings, as if they were doing something wrong—though nothing could be *more* right than he and Rose making love, cuddling afterward, and making each other laugh.

Gently, he rubbed her knee and thigh, exposed by the parted robe.

"Did you get enough to eat?" Rose asked. She ran her fingers through the gray hairs on his chest.

A member of the staff had brought them breakfast earlier—fruit, croissants, guava jelly, and piping hot coffee. Only crumbs remained on the breakfast tray resting on the upholstered bench at the foot of the bed. They weren't concerned about staff tipping off their kids. They wouldn't say a word because they understood discretion.

Monica was often at her fiancé's place, and though she had seen Benicio leave the property early one morning and questioned her mother, Rose had given her an adequate answer that must have allayed her suspicions because she never questioned her again.

"I'm full, thank you." He brought her hand to his lips and kissed it. "I'm surprised I had room after that Thanksgiving feast yesterday."

"Oh goodness, everything was delicious. The staff did an excellent job."

"Yes, they did."

"What do you think about Ignacio and Delta getting back together?" Rose asked, her lips close to his ear.

"I've thought long and hard about their relationship, and if he's happy, that is all that matters. I did not like the back and forth when they were younger. I saw the toll it took on Ignacio. He was very hurt. He loved her very much."

"I believe Delta loved him too. Does he still have the ring?"

Ignacio had planned to give Delta his mother's ring, a family heirloom Valentina had promised to the first of her sons to get married. At twenty-one, Ignacio would have been the first, but he and Delta never tied the knot.

"He does."

"I remember when he showed it to us. It's a gorgeous piece of jewelry, with that huge green diamond," Rose remarked.

"Bruno should have been the one to get the ring since he married first, but he didn't have the heart to ask Ignacio for it. I still do not understand why Delta did not meet him that day. Her father is clearly very influential in her life."

Rose murmured her agreement. "She was young. Maybe now she's older and more established in her career, she'll make her own decisions. She can break away from his control. I'm sure she could find someone who can manage her career just as well—or better."

Benicio patted her knee. "It's not easy to break those family bonds, *mi amor*. There's a lot of money involved, which is why her father could be holding on so tightly. I'm sure Delta feels a sense of obligation to her father for funding her career in the early stages. We don't know what sacrifices her parents made to get her to this point. To drop him now that she is successful..." He shook his head. "That could be seen as ungrateful. Or worse, a betrayal."

"That's a good point," Rose murmured.

"She might also be afraid to break free of her father for fear of failing. He has done a good enough job so far. I've seen many actors who started out as children hesitate to break those familial bonds for that very reason. Who else would care for you as much as a parent? But the truth is, oftentimes, those parents can be selfish."

"Do you think her father is one of those kinds of parents?"

"It is hard to say, but the few times I met him, it was clear he is very driven and, at times, tough on her. Which isn't necessarily bad, but..."

"It can become bad."

"*Sí.*"

Benicio shifted and turned onto his side to look at Rose. Her hair hung in messy loose waves around her face. He'd known her so long that he remembered when her hair was all black, without the gray strands that were there now. Her eyes were still soft and dark brown, but wrinkles had crept into the corners over the years. Yet every time he looked at her, he saw the young, single mother he had run into in the supermarket parking lot. From that moment, he had been smitten.

"We need to take a trip together, just the two of us."

"Where to?" she asked, her smile indulgent.

"The Loire Valley, of course, like we discussed months ago. Back to France, for those delicious croissants."

Her eyes lit up, her excitement palpable. "Really?"

"Of course. Did you think I was joking when I said it?"

She squealed and flung her arms around him. Laughing, Benicio pulled her on top of him and held her tight.

Her eyes smiled into his. "Winter. In the Loire Valley. The two of us."

"Yes," Benicio whispered. "I have to check my schedule, but I would love to go. We could take our time and visit the different châteaux and do whatever else we desire. Just the two of us." He tucked her hair behind her right ear.

"You're sure?" She was smiling, but her eyes searched his face.

"I am. You were right. The life of stress and limitations is for a younger man. It's time to enjoy myself and relax. Thiago is doing a fine job so far."

"So more of this? Because we're not getting any younger. I want us to enjoy our years together."

Benicio frowned. "*Dios, mi amor. Eso es tan morboso.*"

"I'm not trying to be morbid." She brushed his beard with the back of her hand.

Benicio smiled softly and traced her bottom lip with the tip of his finger. "It's not easy for me, you know."

"I know," she said softly.

"I'm not like you, Rosa. You have your garden, your family, and soon two more little ones to keep you busy."

"They're your family too," Rose pointed out.

"Not in the same way. Work is all I have known. Since I was a boy and landed my first acting role. What will I do with myself if I don't work?"

"*Live.* Travel. Spend time with those grandchildren you mentioned. Spend time with *me.*"

He heard the faint tremor in her voice. The pleading he had ignored in the past until she felt she had no choice but to end their marriage. Up until the divorce papers had arrived, he'd believed in his heart that she would change her mind, and they would reconcile.

Now that they were together again, he couldn't imagine losing her for a second time. He couldn't hurt her like that again, making her feel unimportant when, in fact, she was the center of his universe. His world had been off-kilter ever since their marriage ended, and only by staying in touch and remaining amicable had he been able to maintain some semblance of normalcy without losing his mind.

He examined her left hand, hating how empty it looked. One day they would remarry, and she would put her rings back on her finger where they belonged.

"Spending time with you would be the best part," he admitted.

"If you hate taking time off, you could work part-time or act as a consultant."

Her voice ended on a hopeful, upbeat note. Her suggestion was better than in the past, which had been all or nothing. This time, there was the possibility of compromise. She understood how difficult it would be for him to walk away from the company he had built. But he could easily imagine taking time off and having more flexibility to participate in other activities.

"Maybe I will learn a new hobby," he said.

"That would be nice."

He smoothed his hand down the curve of her back to rest on her bottom. "I'll talk to Thiago, *but* understand we're in a transition period. If he needs me..."

"I understand," she said, a smile brightening her face. She cupped his cheek and kissed him. "You've made me so happy with your decision."

"Your happiness is my priority."

Rose leaned in and kissed him again.

* * *

After a delicious lunch of leftovers, Benicio reluctantly headed to the front door with a container of food in his hand. His other hand was linked with Rose's. She held on to him as if she never wanted to let him go, which was a great boost to his ego.

"I'll see you next week," he said, dropping a kiss on her lips.

"I'll start doing some research for our trip."

He would do whatever it took to keep that happy smile on her face. "Sounds good."

Standing on tiptoe, Rose cupped his bearded cheek and gave him a longer, lingering kiss. "I love you," she whispered.

Benicio rested his forehead against hers and closed his eyes. They had said "I love you" to each other multiple times in recent months, yet each time his heart became impossibly full and filled to overflowing with love and affection for this woman.

"Yo también, te amo, mi amor," he said huskily. After one more kiss, he reluctantly left.

As he was driving along the highway, his phone rang, and the name on the car's screen made one eyebrow lift higher.

What does she want? he asked himself. He must have conjured her up with the conversation about Ignacio.

He answered the call. "Hola, Valentina," Benicio greeted his first ex-wife.

"Hello Benicio, how are you?" she asked, also speaking in Spanish.

"I'm fine," he answered carefully.

Years ago, Valentina had taken his sons from Mexico and moved back to her native Colombia out of spite. Then one day she gave up on being a mother and told him he could bring them to the United States to live with him. A long time passed before they were able to speak to each other in a civil manner, and once their sons became adults, they had no reason to communicate at all. In fact, they rarely did. So this call and her friendly demeanor were a big surprise.

"I'm planning a trip to the States to see my cousins in California. Then I want to stop in Atlanta to see the boys. I was hoping I'd get to see you, too, if you're not too busy."

Benicio frowned. Why would she want to see him? "Maybe. It depends on when you're coming."

"I'll have the details soon, but I hope you can make time for me. We could have dinner or something. You know? Like old times."

Like old times? Their marriage had consisted of frequent explosive arguments that seemed never-ending. What a difference it had been when he met Rose. Her calm, quiet personality was in sharp contrast to the volatility he had been used to.

"Get me the dates, and we'll see."

"I'll try to coincide with the birth of Bruno's baby. I'm very excited to have my first grandchild. You've already had the pleasure of being a grandfather through Rose's children, so I envy you. How is Rose, anyway?"

"She's fine." Benicio kept his answer short on purpose, suspicious of this newer, friendlier Valentina.

"I won't keep you. I'll be in touch when my plans are finalized. I hope you can make time for me. It would be nice to see you, Benicio. It's been a long time. Goodbye."

After the call, several minutes passed before Benicio realized he was not only frowning, he was gripping the steering wheel.

Valentina was up to something, and her coming to town could only mean one thing.

Trouble.

Chapter Twenty-One

Sweat glistened on Ignacio's skin as he fought against the weight pressing down on him. His trainer's voice cut through the thrumming of his pulse.

"Come on, you got this. Three more," Marvin commanded.

The metal bar trembled above Ignacio as his muscles strained under the bench press.

"Two more."

Ignacio pushed through the burning sensation in his arms.

"One more."

With a final surge of strength, he forced the bar upward, teeth clenched with the effort.

"That's it, baby!" Pride rang clear in Marvin's voice as he lifted the bar onto the stand. "Good job!"

Ignacio sat up, drawing deep breaths into his burning lungs, his hair damp with sweat.

"Next time, we'll add more weight. This is getting too easy for you."

"Too easy?" Ignacio echoed incredulously, earning a laugh from his trainer.

"Trust me. At this rate, you'll hit your goal weight in no time."

Ignacio was taking full advantage of the six months before he had to report to the set of his next movie. He needed to bulk up for the upcoming action-thriller, his chance to portray a world-weary ex-soldier convinced by an old friend to protect his sister during a treacherous research trip to the Amazon. With franchise potential spanning three films over the next five to six years, the role promised not only an impressive payday but also merchandising opportunities, allowing him to pursue passion projects in the future where he didn't earn as much.

"How are you feeling about the routine?" Marvin asked.

"It's tough, but I like it." Ignacio rolled his shoulders.

"You've increased your protein intake?"

"Yes, and my calories."

"Good. That'll help you bulk up."

Ignacio's team included a doctor and a nutritionist who worked closely with Maria to ensure he consumed the necessary macros every day to prepare him for the role. Marvin wanted his weight and muscle gain to be gradual.

"I'll see you in a couple of days."

"Thanks," Ignacio said, coming to his feet.

They slapped hands, and then Marvin hauled his duffle bag over his shoulder and left.

Delta was working out too, but with a female trainer. While Delta was in a plank position on a padded mat, Mona stood over her with a timer in hand.

"Keep holding," her trainer said, her voice soothing and encouraging.

Ignacio's appreciative gaze traveled the length of Delta's shapely body in black leggings and a black and gray sports bra that showcased her toned abs.

He picked up a towel and wiped the sweat from his face

and chest, then left the women alone, climbing the stairs to the first floor. In the kitchen, he heard the blender running. Maria was preparing their post-workout smoothies.

"Good workout?" she asked in Spanish.

"Yes. I'm going to feel it tomorrow, that's for sure."

He took a glass bottle filled with homemade electrolyte water from the fridge and took a sip.

"Crystal called while you were working out. She wanted to know if you needed anything before she comes over."

"I can't think of anything."

Ignacio removed a black elastic hair tie from his wrist and pulled his hair into a bun. Then he settled onto one of the stools in front of the large island.

His assistant was coming over later so they could review a couple of scripts his agent had sent. One of them was from a Mexican company. He'd done several films in his native Mexico and had a short-running series as well, but most of his success had been in the States, so he hadn't made a Spanish film in a long time and was especially interested in that one.

Maria placed the green smoothie in front of him. "I'm going out in a few minutes. Delta's smoothie is in the fridge."

"Thanks, Maria."

While he drank his smoothie, he checked his texts. He had received another message from Thiago.

When am I going to get my money?

Thiago had first texted him after Thanksgiving dinner: *You owe me 10k.*

Ignacio had told him to go to hell, but his brother was persistent, which was no surprise. Thiago didn't play about money. Ignacio would pay him eventually, but for now, he enjoyed making him suffer.

He typed a short response: *Never.*

Laughing softly to himself, he imagined his brother's pissed off face when he read the text. He then perused the stories about him and Delta. He used to not care what the magazines and blogs said about him, letting Crystal and his publicist keep track of the latest gossip and news. Nowadays, he was curious because their commentary typically included Delta. As far as he could tell, the stories remained mostly positive. He paused to read an article titled *Run It Back: 10 Couples Who Found Their Way Back Together.*

He and Delta were listed as number six, and the image they had chosen was one they'd posted on their Instagram accounts, both casually dressed in jeans and strolling arm in arm in downtown Atlanta. That night, they had dinner and then went for a walk with their bodyguards following closely behind.

Delta was laughing at something he had said, and he watched her with what could only be described as love in his eyes. Because he was in love with her, though he hadn't come right out and said the words. He doubted he ever stopped loving her, even when he was angry and hurt after she didn't meet him to run away and get married.

If he had to guess, he would say she loved him too, but how could he really know since she hadn't said the words either?

Nonetheless, they lived their lives like any other couple since the night they had made love. Their relationship was no longer fake. Their relationship was very much real. They ate breakfast and dinner together, made love most nights, confided in each other, spent time working out, going to dinner, watching movies in their sweatpants in the theater room, and supporting each other at various promotional events around the country.

Ignacio opened Instagram to see what her social media manager had recently posted. The last photo was of the two of them in Miami for an awards event honoring emerging Latin musicians and actors, where he had been a presenter.

Delta had joined him and posted a photo of the two of them backstage at the table, with her leaning against him and his arm around her shoulders. He wore an all-black ensemble, while she wore a Grecian-inspired dress, her hair piled on top of her head and enhanced with gold twine threaded throughout the dark tresses. Kohl-rimmed eyes gave her an air of mystery, making her gaze more mesmerizing beneath the dim lighting. She looked stunning. Regal. Later, they changed clothes and went dancing at a popular nightclub, and Delta was the perfect partner for one of his favorite activities. They slept late the next day and flew back to Atlanta after brunch.

He laughed softly to himself at the comments under the photo.

You have my man.

Happy for you I guess.

Y'all cute or whatever.

Come outside Delta. I just wanna talk.

Tell him I said hey... and to call me when y'all break up.

Just out here living my fantasy with my man. Rude.

"Hey." Delta waltzed into the kitchen.

He lifted his gaze from the phone. "Hey. Your smoothie's in the fridge."

"Thanks."

His eyes followed her to the refrigerator. The black leggings molded over her ass and hugged her toned thighs. His body stirred with the beginnings of arousal.

Delta blew out a tired breath. "I hate Mona so much," she said, sticking a straw in the container.

"She's good for you."

"She pushes me too hard."

"But it's good for you."

"Yes, the hard work is paying off and increasing my endurance. Blah, blah, blah." She rolled her eyes.

Ignacio grabbed her by one of her ass cheeks and pulled her closer. "I like what I see," he said, gently tapping her ass.

She stepped between his legs. Resting her drink on the island, she looped her arms around his neck. "I like what I see too."

Ignacio smoothed his hands down her back and over the curve of her bottom, filling his palms and squeezing with contentment. "Don't tease me," he murmured.

"I'm not," Delta whispered.

They kissed softly while he continued to cup the fullness of her bottom in the palms of his hands.

The sound of Maria clearing her throat forced them to come up for air.

Delta ducked her head and giggled. "Maria, he won't leave me alone."

Maria settled her purse on her shoulder. "I see two people who will not leave each other alone."

Delta gasped with mock outrage. "Maria! You're supposed to be on my side. He's the instigator. I'm completely innocent."

Ignacio's heart swelled in his chest. Sheer joy lit up her face, and he was pleased to be the reason for her happiness.

"*Ah, sí?*" Maria wagged her finger at them. "I take no sides. I see two guilty people. You two, *siempre besándose.* You leave him alone. You leave her alone. Okay? Now, I go to the store. Behave while I am gone. When I come back, I don't want any more trouble."

"Yes, ma'am," they chorused gravely.

With a knowing smile, the housekeeper left through the side door.

"Stop trying to turn my housekeeper against me. We go way back."

"I thought it was worth a shot." Delta kissed the corner of his mouth, then his jawline.

"This is sexual harassment," he said huskily. His breath caught when she found the sensitive spot behind his ear.

"It's only fair since you harass me all the time." Delta licked his neck. "Salty."

Ignacio buried his face against her soft breasts and pulled her tighter between his legs so she could feel his growing erection.

Delta cupped the back of his head. "Hey."

"Mm?" The sound was muffled against her chest.

Her fingers found the elastic tie and released his hair. "What are you working on later? Maybe we can take it easy tonight and finish those last episodes of *Reacher*?"

Having never seen the show, they started with season one and were now both addicted, threatening each other not to watch any episodes without the other.

"Which episode are we on?" Ignacio asked.

"Six, I think."

"We could finish watching the series tonight, but it'll have to be after Crystal leaves. She's coming by so we can review the scripts my agent sent."

"No problem. We can watch the last episodes afterward. Speaking of scripts, what's the latest on *Wrong*?"

Ignacio moaned softly and temporarily closed his eyes as she used her fingertips to massage his scalp. "King's screenwriter is reviewing the script. He's going to give me his feedback next week."

"Do you think he'll have to rewrite the whole thing?"

"I hope not. I like what we have."

Looking into his eyes, she continued to massage his scalp while he kept his arms wrapped around her waist.

"Can I read it?"

Ignacio frowned. "You want to read my script?"

"Sure. You've seen my music and my poems, but I haven't seen your script."

His hands fell away. "I don't think that's a good idea."

"Why not?"

"Because..." His hesitation hung between them like fog.

Delta tilted her head to the side. "Why don't you want me to read it?"

Ignacio hadn't considered why until that very moment. He wasn't the type to doubt his own abilities. In fact, he was often teased about his big ego, yet he couldn't shake the unease about Delta reading what he had written.

"I'm worried you won't like the story," he admitted.

"Ignacio," she said in a chiding voice.

"You're talented. You're good with words."

"And so are you," she replied.

"No. I'm good at acting. I recite the words other people write and bring them to life."

She placed a hand on her hip. "Aren't you the one who told me that if you don't believe in yourself, why should anyone else?"

"I believe in myself," he said.

"But you think I'll judge your work negatively."

When he didn't reply, she tapped his nose with the tip of her finger. "Silly man. I'm one hundred percent certain I'll like what I read. Let me read it. Please?" She batted her eyelashes.

Laughing, Ignacio shook his head. "You know I can't deny you anything when you look at me like that."

"You can't? Good to know." A serious expression came over her face. "Would you share the script with me?"

"Yes, I will."

This felt like a big deal. He was sharing a piece of himself with her that he hadn't shared before.

A radiant smile bloomed across her face. "Thank you. I promise not to judge."

Ignacio believed her. He trusted her—something he hadn't thought he'd ever do again.

He cupped her cheek. "You're an incredible woman, you know that?"

"And you're an incredible man." She licked his neck. "An incredibly salty man," she whispered.

"You like licking me?" he whispered in her ear.

"Mhmm. You taste good." Her eyes sparkled with mischief.

"My turn." Ignacio hooked his thumb in the waistband of her leggings.

Delta danced away, laughing. "Where exactly are you planning to lick me?"

"My favorite spot," he purred.

Her eyes widened. "You're so nasty."

"*Ven acá, mujer*." He reached for her.

"No!" Delta slapped his hands away and took off running.

"Come here, let me lick you!" Ignacio jumped up and raced after her.

Her squeals and laughter echoed through the house as she fled, and Ignacio bounded up the stairs after her in hot pursuit.

Chapter Twenty-Two

Amazing.

Reclining on the chaise lounge in the reading nook of the owner's suite, Delta hugged the script to her chest and sighed.

Wrong had elicited a deeply emotional response from her—not only because of the wrongful conviction and the time Gideon spent in jail but also because of the fight to clear his name. The rekindled relationship between him and his ex, Samantha, and his connection with the son he had never known were particularly poignant. She was eager to see how Ignacio would bring those moments to life on the big screen.

Standing, she stretched her hands above her head. She had been sitting for a long while. The script had been as engrossing as a novel, and she hadn't wanted to stop until she reached the very end. With the pages held against her body, she went down the hall to Ignacio's office and knocked before entering. Crystal sat cross-legged on the sofa with her iPad while Ignacio sat in his chair with his feet propped up on the desk.

Before he could ask her opinion, Delta said, "*Wrong* is a masterpiece."

"Wow," Crystal said.

"A masterpiece?" Ignacio sounded doubtful, but his face said he was very pleased by the compliment.

"It's such a great story," Delta said, placing the pages on his desk.

"But..." Ignacio prompted.

She hesitated, searching for the right words. "At first, I didn't understand what you meant by saying something was missing. I loved everything. The dialogue, the characters are complex and likable, and the antagonists create great friction and external conflict. I swear, I wanted to strangle the guard and Samantha's father! As it's written, I think the script would make a great film, but I agree—something is missing, and I think I know what it is."

Crystal sat forward.

"What?" Ignacio dropped his feet to the floor.

"You need a twist. Something to shock the audience at the end."

"A twist," he said slowly. Then he nodded and sprang to his feet. "You're right. Everything ties up too neatly."

"Exactly."

Stroking his jaw, he paced the room. "A twist. What could it be?" he murmured.

Crystal stifled a yawn, but Ignacio heard her.

"Crystal, go home," he said.

"Huh? No, I want to help."

"You've done enough, and you're flying to Amsterdam to pick up that package for me tomorrow. Go."

"But—"

"*Go.*" Ignacio's voice was firm and authoritative, a tone he seldom took with Crystal.

"You're not the boss of me," she pouted, unfolding her legs and standing.

"I'm literally your boss," Ignacio reminded her.

His assistant picked up her belongings while grumbling. "I'm leaving, but I don't like it. At least keep me posted. I want to know what you decide to do."

"I'll let you know about the changes. Have a safe trip."

She glared at him. "Bye," she said in a petulant voice.

"Bye," Delta said.

Crystal waved and quietly closed the door behind her.

"Sometimes she loses her mind and thinks she's in charge," Ignacio said.

"She's not?" Delta teased, taking a seat in front of his desk.

"Very funny. Now, where were we? Oh, the twist."

"Right."

They spent the next thirty minutes brainstorming and tossing around ideas while Ignacio paced the room, every so often running his fingers through his curls in frustration. She wished she could help him. A twist would improve the story, but she didn't know what the twist should be.

Suddenly, Ignacio swung in her direction, his gray eyes lighting up. "I have it!"

"Okay, tell me."

"What if the senator was somehow involved?"

"The senator that Samantha is married to?"

He nodded.

Delta mulled the idea for a few seconds. "Go on."

"So, the senator knew Gideon was innocent all along but covered it up."

Delta chewed the corner of her mouth. "Okay, but why? He needs a really good reason."

"Why? Why?" Ignacio started pacing again, and her eyes

followed his movement in the small room. The low-slung jeans and tight gray T-shirt looked great on his physique, which was filling out thanks to training with Marvin. His body was ripped, his biceps larger and barely contained by the shirt. She couldn't wait to climb on top of him in bed later and have his hands touch her everywhere while his glorious, wicked mouth dragged her to the edge of sanity. Her body hummed with anticipation.

Ignacio abruptly stopped. "Because the real culprit was a donor's son."

Delta's mouth fell open. "I love that idea."

"By hiding the information, the senator allowed an innocent man to go to jail, protected the guilty party, and secured continuous money for his senatorial campaign."

"Not to mention cleared the way for him to pursue the heroine."

"You would think about that."

"It's important for the romantic subplot," Delta reasoned.

"True," Ignacio said with a laugh. "So you really like the twist?"

"I think it's brilliant. Moviegoers will be sympathetic toward him because the poor guy is being shoved aside after he's been a loyal husband to Samantha and a good stepfather to her son."

"Exactly."

"The whole time, he's a monster who allowed an innocent man to go to prison for a crime he didn't commit. I think you got it."

"I think I got it." Ignacio looked at her with appreciation in his eyes. "Thank you."

"I didn't do much. You came up with the idea."

"Because you pointed out what was missing." He sat on the sofa, where Crystal had been sitting earlier. "Before I reach out to David, I'll rewrite those parts and then send the pages to him for feedback."

David was the screenwriter King had assigned to work with Ignacio.

"Does directing and writing give you as much excitement as acting?" Delta asked.

"Acting will always be my first love. I can't believe people pay me to pretend, but filmmaking produces a different type of excitement in me."

"I can tell. You're passionate about it. I think we're both lucky that we get to do work we're passionate about."

"Despite the drawbacks," he muttered.

"What do you consider a drawback?"

"The usual stuff that people in our industry complain about. We have a lot of perks but very little privacy, every decision picked apart by the press and fans, and the media is constantly jumping to conclusions. I can't have lunch with a member of the opposite sex without people assuming that we're dating."

Delta nodded her agreement. "I hate the need for constant security. I kind of liked not being noticed after my album didn't do so well. But then the drawback was—"

"Your album didn't do well."

"Exactly."

They both laughed.

"You know what else I hate? I mean, it's a small thing, but... I miss birthday celebrations."

"What do you mean?" Ignacio asked.

"I used to love celebrating my birthday. My parents made a big deal out of it because my aunts died so young. 'Every birthday is a blessing,' my dad used to say. We didn't always have parties, and when we did, they weren't a big production, but it was nice having someone else do the planning, you know?

Seeing how King Brockwell and his family planned the party for his mother made me think about those days. I don't need a big to-do. Small and meaningful is just as beautiful, in my opinion. Like the time you arranged for a candlelit dinner on the beach for my birthday. Do you remember? You had a private chef prepare my favorite dishes, and we had a picnic under the stars. That was the last time anyone planned a birthday celebration for me."

"You haven't had anyone plan a birthday party for you—or anything since then? That was ages ago. We must have been what... eighteen?"

"Nineteen." They were both working for her twentieth birthday, and for her twenty-first birthday, she went on a girls' trip to Mexico. He met her there at the tail end of the trip to celebrate.

Once she became famous, her friends would show up to the dinners or outings she arranged, but no one took the initiative to make her feel special. As she became wealthier, people expected her to host extravagant parties and go all out, which meant she had to organize the event and cover the costs. She missed the parties from when she was a kid. They were magical and filled with love, and she felt special each and every time. It was her day.

"We need to do something special for your birthday next year," Ignacio said.

"I didn't mention it for you to do anything," Delta said with a laugh. "It was just an observation that when you get to a certain level, people expect you to throw the party. I guess it's because they think it has to be something big, you know? Not realizing it's the thought that counts."

"Which is why I'm going to throw you a party next year," he said with conviction.

"Ignacio."

"You don't want a party?"

Delta paused, struck by a thought she had been avoiding. "Will we be together then?" she asked softly.

He looked deeply into her eyes. "I hope so. I still love you, Delta, and I want to be with you."

"Nacio." Her voice cracked.

Hearing the love of her life say "I still love you" made every fear, every doubt, every ache melt away. It was like returning home after being lost for years and feeling safe and cherished.

Ignacio came to where she was seated and sank onto his haunches before her. He took her hand and kissed it. "This isn't fake. This isn't a performance. The only performance—my greatest performance—was pretending I wasn't obsessed with you."

"I love you too," Delta said, her voice quivering. All the other men since they broke up had been stand-ins, mere substitutes. Her heart and body belonged to Ignacio. Always had. She had basically been waiting for the day he came back into her life and reclaimed them.

"I tried multiple times to convince myself that I didn't care about you, that I didn't miss you. I even wrote a song about it. The title is 'I Don't Miss You.'" She let out an embarrassed laugh.

"I guess the song is the opposite of that?"

"Sort of. One day I might share the words with you." Her lower lip trembled. "I love you so much. I'm so sorry that I—"

"Shh." He kissed her knuckles. "I don't care. We're here. Together. We can do this, Delta. Right this time. Yes?"

She nodded. "Yes."

Ignacio stood and lifted her from the chair. She wrapped her arms and legs around him, moaning at their languid, heartfelt kiss. In their bedroom, they quickly disposed of their clothes and then reached for each other, touching and caressing with utmost urgency—both of them filled with uncontrollable, all-consuming desire.

Delta cried out at the joining of their bodies. She arched into him, each thrust taking her higher. When his fingers closed around her throat, her nails sank into his ass as the lack of oxygen made her dizzy, and her eyes rolled back in her head.

Over and over, he drove into her while her sobs of ecstasy filled the room. He whispered words of hunger, love, and desperation against her skin, each pump of his hips etching his devotion into her very soul.

Chapter Twenty-Three

The annual Simmonds Foundation Charity Gala always brought out Hollywood's elite to raise money for LA's underprivileged youth. Ignacio was not usually lucky enough to attend but came whenever he could to support the cause.

The white limo pulled up to the venue, and the chauffeur opened the back door. Ignacio exited first, dressed in a black tux, his hair slicked back and pulled into a man bun at the nape. He extended a hand to help Delta out of the vehicle. She left her stole on the car seat, but they wouldn't remain in the chilly night air for long.

Delta wore a shimmery black sleeveless gown. Her hair was parted in the middle and pulled into a sleek bun, as well, and Harry Winston diamonds dangled from her ears and adorned her slender wrists. Because of the value of the pieces she wore, the jeweler had provided extra security to shadow her and Ignacio this evening.

When they walked onto the red carpet, cheers erupted

from the onlookers lucky enough to have tickets to be in the stands overlooking the entrance, and camera bulbs flashed in quick succession as photographers captured the event for their various publications. Media personnel shouted their names in an effort to get their attention for the perfect shot.

"Delta, this way!"

"Who are you wearing?"

"Delta, over here, beautiful!"

"Smile for me, Delta!"

"Ignacio, this way!"

They turned and smiled, posing for the cameras. Delta's publicist slipped behind to fix the train of her dress before darting away. For a few minutes, he and Delta separated, allowing the photographers to capture individual photos of them. During those brief moments, Ignacio had a hard time concentrating on his poses. His eyes were constantly drawn to Delta. She sparkled like the jewels in her ears and around her wrists.

They held hands again and continued down the line before entering the venue. Inside the dimly lit interior, they were greeted by other celebrities. Hugs and plenty of air-kisses were exchanged, and in between, entertainment reporters asked questions about their upcoming projects.

After a round of interviews, they settled into their chairs for the program, which lasted a little over an hour. Then loud music drew them to a room next door, and they hit the dance floor with the rest of the guests. Much later, with their arms entwined around each other, they moved to the beat of a slow-tempo song.

"I'm starving," Ignacio murmured in Delta's ear.

"Me too. Let's find some food."

He nodded his agreement and led her out of the room to

where the Simmonds Foundation members had set up drinks and heavy hors d'oeuvres for guests. As they headed toward one of the tables, Vincent, his friend and a British actor, stopped Ignacio with a hand to his chest.

"Ignacio, mate, how the hell are you?"

"Vincent, good to see you." Ignacio grabbed his hand, and they went in for a man hug, clapping each other on the back.

"It's been far too long, hasn't it? Not my fault, though. You've been keeping a low profile—no parties, no wild nights. Can't say I blame you, mind. I wouldn't go anywhere either if I had this stunning creature to keep me occupied." He turned his gaze to Delta.

"This is Delta—"

"No need for introductions, mate. I know exactly who she is. Delta J." Vincent took her hand and brushed a kiss across the back of it. "Vincent Ryan. An absolute pleasure to meet you."

"Nice to meet you, Vincent," she said.

Vincent flung an arm around Ignacio's neck. "I'm not as famous as this bloke here, but I'm working on it. One day, I'll reach his level—mark my words." He stepped back, giving Ignacio an exaggerated once-over. "Bloody hell, you're built like an ox now."

Ignacio chuckled easily. "You know how it is. Getting ready for my next role."

"Ah, yes. The public has no idea how hard we work, do they?" He posed the question to Delta, but before she could respond, he said to Ignacio, "So, when's the next shindig? Got my dancing shoes at the ready."

"Hard to say. My schedule is packed for the foreseeable future," Ignacio hedged.

He had no plans to throw a party anytime soon, and if he did, it wouldn't be like they were in the past. Oddly enough, he didn't miss the all-night partying and drinking. Something else he didn't miss—smoking. He hadn't craved a cigarette in a long time.

Vincent scoffed. "A busy schedule never stopped you before." He winked and nudged Ignacio with his elbow. "Ah well, I suppose I'll just have to wait for my invite, yeah? You've still got my number?"

"Of course."

"Brilliant. Oh, before I forget, congrats on getting *Wrong* funded. I guess that's one of the reasons you'll be busy in the coming months, yeah? Miss Delta J, it was a delight to meet you. You're more breathtaking in person than in your photos. I'll catch you both later."

When he walked away, Delta said, "He's got a lot of energy."

"That's him being calm. He's damn near out of control when he gets liquor in his system. At my last party, he was tossing furniture."

"What?" Delta's eyes widened, and she covered her mouth as she laughed.

"He's a good guy, but when he gets drunk..." Ignacio shook his head. "There's a small crowd over there. That's probably where the good food is."

"Definitely," Delta agreed.

They moved in that direction.

"Hey, there's Leo Hargrove," Ignacio said, using his chin to point out the producer, now executive, who had worked on Delta's first album.

Leo had also produced the soundtrack for *Sleeping Poets*. Dressed in a fitted tux with his salt-and-pepper hair neatly trimmed, Leo looked every bit the successful music mogul. This was the first time Ignacio had seen him in L.A. Leo lived in Atlanta, and that's where he had run into him a couple of times over the years.

Delta's small hand reached for and gripped Ignacio's, and she pressed closer to his side, forcing him to halt his stride. Surprised, his eyebrows drew together, and he turned to her. Her chest rose and fell quickly because her breathing had accelerated. And she was staring at Leo.

What the…?

His gaze returned to the older man, who was now approaching them with a friendly smile. Delta drew even closer, as if trying to make herself invisible. Her hand tightened to the point of crushing his fingers. Her nails dug into his skin.

Leo stopped in front of them. "Delta, Ignacio, I didn't know the two of you were here tonight. How are you doing this evening?"

Ignacio's stomach churned as realization dawned on him. Before he had time to think, he reacted. His hand slipped from Delta's, and he punched Leo square in the mouth. He crashed into a snacks table and tumbled to the floor. Guests jumped out of the way, gasping and screaming in horror.

Ignacio's jaw was clenched so hard he'd probably end up grinding down his molars. Bending to Leo, who had blood dripping from his lip, he grabbed the older man's lapels. Leo swung an arm across his face in a defensive move, but Ignacio didn't hit him again.

He whispered in a growl, "Don't you ever come near her again, you piece of shit, or I'll kill you with my bare hands."

They locked eyes, and the fact that Leo didn't demand to know what he was talking about told Ignacio everything he needed to know. *He* was the one who had violated Delta when she was a minor and had the audacity to approach her as if nothing had happened.

Ignacio stood upright and glared at Leo on the floor, fighting the urge to stomp his head with the heel of his shoe. He straightened his tux and then took Delta's hand. Their security closed around them as they walked away, with everyone staring and whispering to each other about what had occurred.

Behind him, Ignacio heard Leo calming the masses. "Folks, it's okay. Just a big misunderstanding."

He almost went back to hit him again, but he'd done enough and didn't want to traumatize Delta any more. She continued to hold tight to his hand as they left the venue.

"Call the driver," he said in a clipped voice to Randall. Right away, his bodyguard pulled out his phone.

Beside him, tiny tremors rocked Delta's frame. Ignacio placed an arm around her shoulders, and she snuggled closer. After a few minutes, the shaking subsided, and her breathing normalized.

When the driver pulled up, Randall and Ava ushered them into the limo before closing the door. Ava sat up front, and Randall followed behind in a car with the rest of the security.

Ignacio rolled up the partition and turned to Delta. He held her hand. "Are you okay?"

She swallowed and turned hollowed-out eyes on him. "You shouldn't have done that," she whispered in a tremulous voice.

"I'm not apologizing."

"I don't want you to apologize, you just shouldn't have done that. He's going to retaliate, Ignacio."

"There is nothing he can do to you," he said confidently.

Slowly, she shook her head. "You're wrong, and I'm talking about you. Do you really think he's going to let you get away with knocking him down in front of a bunch of people? Cameras were flashing, and everyone saw. He's going to get his revenge on you—and me." Her eyes were wide and terrified.

"I won't let him hurt you," he promised, but he didn't think she believed him.

"How did you know?" she asked. "I never told you his name."

"I had enough information based on what you said, and... you became different when he approached." He kissed her hand. "*Mi amor*, he can't hurt you or me. I won't let him."

She trailed a hand down his jaw, and a sad smile touched her lips. He wished he had hit Leo again.

"Why didn't you tell your parents? There must have been other times during the years when you ran into him, and they probably didn't understand when your behavior changed."

She lowered her gaze to her lap.

"You have to be willing to accept help, *mi amor*. You can't do everything on your own."

"Believe me, I do accept help—when it's offered."

The sadness in her eyes called out to him, and then he read the truth and cold disbelief enveloped him.

"They knew," he whispered.

Slowly, she nodded, and her bottom lip trembled.

Ignacio muttered a curse and squeezed her hand. "Delta..."

"They left me with him," she whispered, her voice trembling. "It was the price we had to pay—"

"*We?*" he growled in a low voice, his eyes boring into her in disbelief. "You were the one who suffered. Not them. *You* paid the price, and they reaped the reward."

He muttered another expletive and tightened his jaw, wanting to dispel the truth but knowing it wasn't uncommon for parents and guardians to "sacrifice" their children for money and fame.

Delta rested her head on his shoulder, and he closed his arms in a protective circle around her.

Bile rose in his throat at the thought of her, only sixteen years old, being left alone with Leo Fucking Hargrove and then having to work with him on an album after the fact. All with the full knowledge of her parents.

He'd never been so angry.

Then he thought about Eddie J. What kind of father would allow such a heinous crime to be committed against his daughter?

Fucking scum.

Ignacio had never wanted to kill anyone more in his life.

Chapter Twenty-Four

She was going to be sick.

Delta had known the backlash was coming, but she hadn't expected Leo to move so quickly. The texted photos were an unmistakable threat.

With her feet rooted to the floor of the bedroom she shared with Ignacio, she stared down at the screen of her phone, holding the device with trembling fingers. Leo had sent two photos of her sixteen-year-old self with bare shoulders to indicate her nakedness without showing her nude body.

As she watched, another text came through. This one contained only words. This time, the nausea won. She raced into the bathroom and dropped the phone on the counter, barely reaching the toilet in time to throw up. The contents of her stomach splashed into the water.

When she was finished, she wiped her mouth, tears brimming in her eyes, hugging the bowl like a woman dealing with the aftermath of a night spent drinking. She wasn't sure how much time passed, but that's how Ignacio found her when he returned home from his morning run.

He dropped to his haunches. "Delta, what's wrong?" Panic filled his voice.

She didn't know how to answer.

Ignacio smoothed her hair from her face with a gentle hand. "What's wrong, *mi amor*? Talk to me."

"I told you he would—he would retaliate."

He knew right away who she was referring to, and his lips firmed. "What happened?"

"There's a tape." Delta sniffed.

"A tape? I don't understand."

She roughly brushed the tears from her cheeks. "He taped me. I had no idea he was recording what happened."

Ignacio stared at her in silence. "How did you find out?"

She pointed at her phone on the counter. "He sent messages."

Ignacio retrieved the phone and then returned to her. She took the device and showed him the photos and the text. "The photos must be stills from the video. He doesn't come right out and admit that he filmed me, but he makes it clear in the text that a video exists."

"I can't believe he sent these to you." Ignacio's voice was tight with barely restrained anger, his brows furrowed as he stared at the screen. His grip on the phone was so tense she half-expected it to crack. "But no matter what he threatens, he won't release a video of you."

"Why do you think he won't?" Delta demanded.

"Because if he did, he would incriminate himself. You were a minor, and what he did to you was evil and illegal. He would never want the general public to find out."

She let out a brittle laugh, hollow and filled with pain. "You don't know that, Ignacio."

"I do."

He reached for her, but she recoiled, scooting backward

until she hit the wall. She drew in her legs and folded her arms tightly across them in an effort to make herself smaller. She wanted to disappear.

"You're wrong. He doesn't care," she whispered.

Ignacio exhaled, dragging a hand down his face. "Delta, listen to me. If he releases the video, he would be in a lot of trouble. Trust me." He spoke in a low, coaxing voice, as if trying to talk someone off a ledge.

"Trust you? I trusted you when I told you what happened to me, and you—" Her voice broke with emotion. "You attacked him in public, Ignacio."

His face twisted, contrition flickering in his eyes. "I wasn't thinking." His voice was hoarse and full of regret.

"I don't know what to do. He's threatening to tell everyone that I slept my way to the top. I don't know what to do. I don't..." She started shaking again.

This time, when he reached for her, she didn't move away. She allowed him to pull her into his chest. Sobbing on his shoulder, she clung to him, crying her eyes out.

"I'll fix it. I promise, he won't hurt you anymore. I'll do whatever I have to do." He smoothed her hair as she continued to cry.

Delta lost track of time, and when she finally stopped crying, his shirt was soaked. She moved away from Ignacio, rinsed out her mouth, and washed her face. Ignacio watched her in silence, sensing she no longer wanted to be touched.

Without saying a word, she returned to the bedroom and climbed into bed. Maybe she would stay there all day. Ignacio climbed in behind her.

Anxiety remained in the pit of her stomach like a stone, but having his comforting presence in the bed made her feel better, though she didn't want him to touch her at the moment. She huddled under the covers, wrapping her arms around herself until she fell asleep.

Delta woke to darkness. The blackout curtains were drawn tight, blocking out the sun.

For a moment, she lay still, her body heavy with exhaustion. She reached blindly for her phone on the nightstand, her fingers closing around it with sluggish effort. The screen's glow stung her eyes, and she squinted.

Eight thirty-eight in the morning. Wednesday. She had a flight in a few hours.

She pressed a hand to her forehead. The past few days were a blur of long hours—waiting, dreading, bracing for Leo's next move. Sleep had been difficult as worst-case scenarios played on a loop in her head. What would he do next to punish her for Ignacio's actions?

She rolled out of bed with effort and shuffled to the bathroom, splashing cold water on her face, which did little to energize her. She stared at her reflection. Her makeup artist would have to work a miracle. All she saw was a hollow-eyed woman with dull skin, the strain from Leo's threats etched into her features.

After she finished her morning routine, she opened the curtains and allowed light to flood the bedroom. Behind her, she heard the door crack open.

Ignacio entered. "Hey, you're awake," he said in a soft voice.

He carried a tray in his hands and placed it on the table beside the bed. The tray contained a small plate of cut-up fruit and a glass of water. A simple, light breakfast because she hadn't been able to eat much since she received the messages.

"How are you feeling?" His voice was grave and weighted with concern.

"Horrible," Delta admitted. After a pause, she continued. "I've been thinking about what I said in the bathroom the other day, and I don't blame you for what Leo did."

"Don't worry about it."

"You're being too nice."

Ignacio rubbed the back of his neck. "I'm not going to apologize for hitting him. Frankly, I wish I could have done more, but I understand your feelings. Now you have to deal with the fallout. But you shouldn't have to worry about Leo. You should be focusing on your trip—the interviews and your promo events."

Delta sighed and sank onto the edge of the bed. He was right, but she no longer looked forward to the nine-day trip to New York. With the album finished and the release date set, pre-release promotion had begun. Videos of her in the studio had been distributed to the media to generate excitement, and her schedule was packed with interviews and photo shoots in the coming weeks. She dreaded facing the media and having to force smiles and answer questions. She felt as if what lay ahead would suffocate her.

This should be the exciting part. The music was finished, the release date locked in, and the momentum building. Normally, she would be eager to share the stories behind the songs, joke and laugh during interviews, and bask in the energy of it all. Promote herself and the music. Instead, all she wanted to do was crawl into bed and hide under the covers indefinitely.

Leo could strike again at any moment. Even if he didn't release the video as he threatened, there were other ways he could hurt her. He could sabotage her release, have marketing cut the promotion budget, or pull strings to ensure the press coverage turned against her. There were countless ways he could make her life miserable.

And all she could do was wait.

"Maybe I should talk to him," Delta murmured, searching Ignacio's face for any sign that he thought it was a good idea. Maybe she could reason with Leo and find a way to make this all go away.

"No." His response was immediate and decisive. He clasped her hands between his, his grip warm and steady. "I don't want you wasting another second thinking about him. Go to New York and focus on what matters—your album, your interviews. Walk into every room like you own it, promote the hell out of your music, and then meet with A&R and blow them away with the recordings of your new songs. Impress the hell out of them so they have to say yes to including them on the album."

She smiled weakly. His words were meant to reassure her, but worry continued to gnaw at her.

Ignacio's gaze held hers, steady and unwavering. "I'm going to fix this mess I made," he said, his voice resolute.

"How?" Delta asked.

"Let me worry about that."

"You make it sound simple, but we both know it's not."

Ignacio squeezed her hands gently. "You have to trust me, okay?"

Trust was difficult when the ground beneath her felt like it could collapse at any moment, but Ignacio hadn't steered her wrong yet.

"Okay."

She let go of his hands and reached for the tray he'd brought in earlier. The fruit was fresh, cut into neat pieces, and though she didn't have much of an appetite, she forced herself to eat some. Ignacio watched her with quiet intensity as she did.

Later, Delta took a shower. Then she packed her bags and double-checked her itinerary, though she knew it by heart. Ignacio stayed in the room with her, sitting in one of the chairs, his legs extended straight out before him as he silently observed her.

When the phone beeped with a message from the driver, she took a deep breath. Time to go.

She zipped up her luggage. While Ignacio took both bags—her carry-on and the wheeled suitcase—she slipped her arms into her winter coat.

"Feels strange," she remarked as they descended the stairs to the first level.

"What does?"

"Leaving and not knowing what's waiting for me when I land," Delta admitted.

Maybe her fears were irrational, but they weren't going anywhere.

Ignacio placed the bags on the floor in the foyer. His fingers brushed her cheek as he tucked a strand of hair behind her ear. "What did I say earlier?"

"Focus on my interviews and promo events."

"Exactly. I'll handle everything here." He cupped her face, his thumb tracing the line of her cheek. He lowered his head. "Do you think you can follow my instructions?"

She smiled for the first time in days. "Yes, sir."

"Good."

He pressed his lips to hers. The kiss was slow and lingering, a goodbye filled with promises. When they finally parted, she wrapped her arms around his waist.

Rubbing her back, Ignacio kissed her temple. "Go, before I change my mind and keep you here."

Delta let out a shaky laugh. "That might not be so bad," she said, but she released him and moved toward the front door.

Ignacio followed her to the black sedan idling in the driveway. As she slid into the back seat, he placed her luggage in the trunk.

Then he came up to the window. He leaned in, and she puckered her lips, happily accepting another quick kiss from him.

"Bye, baby," she whispered.

"Bye, *mi amor*. Good luck."

The car pulled away, and she glanced back, watching Ignacio as he stood in the driveway, his hands buried in the pockets of his jeans.

He promised he would take care of everything.

She decided to trust him.

Chapter Twenty-Five

Ignacio left his bodyguard downstairs and took the private elevator to the top floor where his father's office was located. Benicio's executive assistant waved him through, and he knocked on the door before entering.

"*¿Qué pasa, papá?*" he said.

Benicio was standing behind his desk and glanced up. He switched to Spanish too. "Hi, son. Give me a second."

"Take your time." He appreciated his father being willing to meet with him in the middle of the day on such short notice. He was busy, not only with work but also with the transition of Thiago take over the business.

He sauntered over to the sitting area, where two leather couches flanked a table with a couple of business magazines on the surface. "Will Thiago be moving into this office?"

"No, and I need a place to work when I come in occasionally. He brought in designers to combine two offices, and they're already working on the renovations."

"I bet it's much different from this."

"Much," his father agreed with a laugh.

Benicio's taste ran more traditional, with dark wood finishes on all the furniture, a built-in bookcase, and a credenza. Knowing Thiago, he'd want a modern aesthetic to match his office in Brazil.

Benicio gathered a few documents from his desk, placed them inside the top drawer, and then locked it. "I'm starving," he said, picking up his charcoal jacket from the back of his leather chair and slipping his arms into the sleeves.

"Did you decide where you wanted to eat?"

Benicio buttoned his jacket as he moved from behind the desk. "I thought we could walk to a restaurant down the street. There's a great little Ethiopian place that I've eaten at twice in the past month."

"Sounds good to me. I haven't had Ethiopian cuisine in a long time." Ignacio fell into step beside him.

They took the elevator to the first floor and exited a side door onto the street. As they passed by the front of the building, Ignacio told Randall he didn't have to come and to wait in the car.

Ignacio had pulled his hair into a bun and wore a black cap low on his face. In the hustle and bustle of downtown Atlanta, he didn't anticipate anyone paying him any attention.

As both men strolled down the sidewalk, Benicio asked, "What happened the other night between you and the music executive?"

"Nothing."

"Nothing? The news said you punched him and stomped him. That sounds like something Thiago would do, not you."

"I didn't stomp him, but I should have." His publicist had issued statements on his behalf to calm the frenzy after he hit Leo and insisted that he steer clear of the media and use the standard *No comment* response if asked about the incident.

He didn't care about himself. His only regret was that he

had caused Delta more trauma. When he found her on the floor in the bathroom and she looked up at him with tear-filled eyes, the world had collapsed around him. He had seen nothing but pain and wanted to stop it. If he could, he would kill Leo Hargrove, but instead of murder, he was going to keep his promise to Delta and fix the mess he had made.

"And why should you have stomped him?" Benicio asked.

"He's a vile human being, and a beatdown was long overdue."

Ignacio changed the subject, and he and his father chatted about mundane topics until they arrived at the restaurant. Inside, the waitress led them through a maze of black-stained teakwood tables. The afternoon sunlight filtered through the window, creating a stark contrast to the restaurant's dimly lit interior. Ignacio slid onto a booth seat and picked up the menu but decided to let his father order for them both since he'd eaten there multiple times.

When the server left them alone, he folded his arms on the table.

"Are you ready to tell me why you wanted to have this meeting? When you said you needed to talk right away, I was concerned."

"I have a problem, and I need your help figuring something out."

"Tell me about it."

Their male server approached and placed their club sodas on the table.

When he left, Ignacio leaned toward his father. "I have a friend who has a problem—"

"A friend?" His father arched a white eyebrow.

"Not me, if that's what you're thinking. The problem is really someone else's." He had to convince his father of this, or he'd be concerned. Despite them all being adults, his parents still worried about them and were willing to help whenever problems arose.

"Okay, go ahead," Benicio said, pouring his water into a glass filled with ice.

"As I mentioned, my friend has a problem. Something happened to them a long time ago. It was a crime, and the person who committed the crime against them has a video and recently threatened to release it."

His father frowned. "Isn't the person who committed the crime worried about the release of this video? It would incriminate them, wouldn't it?"

"It would," Ignacio confirmed. "But the victim has an irrational fear of being exposed and refuses to accept that. They think the perpetrator may release the video, or parts of it, to make them look bad. They're terrified of this happening."

Benicio scratched his beard. "That's a tough position to be in. They're a victim being victimized again."

"Exactly." Ignacio lowered his voice. "I have an idea of how to help them, but I'm not sure where to turn for this help."

"What did you have in mind?"

"I need to get the video."

Benicio nodded slowly. "That's the best option. Is there any chance there are multiple copies?"

"Possibly, and if there are, we'd need to get them too. Do you know of anyone who could handle this type of situation? I don't care about the cost."

His father studied him for a fraction of a second before asking, "You're footing the bill for this... friend?"

"Yes."

"I see. Well, I have an idea of someone who could help—maybe. Your friend's problem sounds like the kind of thing they could assist with, but you'd have to talk to them and find out for sure. I don't want to get your hopes up."

"Okay," Ignacio said, anxiously awaiting the information.

Benicio also leaned in. "Oscar and Sylvie's son-in-law works for a company of ex-military people or something like that. To be honest, I'm not sure, but I know they're good at what they do, and I took several cards from Oscar in case I ever find myself in a bind."

He reached into his pocket, removed his wallet, and pulled out a card, which he slid across the table.

Ignacio picked it up. "Tyrone Evers, The Cordoba Agency."

Benicio nodded. "He's their son-in-law, a former cop. Anyway, the company itself is a security and investigative firm, but Oscar hinted they could handle situations no one else can."

"This might be exactly what I'm looking for."

"Give Tyrone a call and see what he says. He'll let you know if they can help or not."

"Thanks. I knew you'd have an answer."

"It's nice to still be needed," his father said with a low chuckle.

Ignacio tucked the card into the front pocket of his jeans. "You'll always be needed."

Benicio smiled. "So, tell me what's going on with your film project."

They spent the rest of the meal discussing his ideas and the decision to add the twist after Delta's suggestion, which Benicio agreed was a good idea.

When the food arrived, they indulged in huge platters of meat seasoned with onions, peppers, and a blend of spices. On the side were potato stew, mushroom stew, and rolls of teff injera.

Finally, they left the restaurant, Ignacio carrying a container with a meal for his bodyguard. As they strolled up the sidewalk, he finally broached another subject that had been on his mind since he learned about the role Delta's parents played in giving that monster access to her.

"Father, I want to thank you. Not only for the help you just provided but for how you protected me when I was younger. You never let me travel alone and wanted to be involved in every aspect of my acting career. I hated that shit."

Benicio chuckled. "Yes, and I remember how upset you always were."

"I understand now, and I understand why you said no to certain events. At the time, I couldn't grasp why you'd have me miss out on opportunities that could help my career, and I didn't care when you explained there would be other opportunities."

Though he'd benefited from having actor parents, when he was younger, he'd assumed he could be further along in his career if his father hadn't limited his options. His parents often argued about his career because his mother believed he was old enough and mature enough to handle more of the industry, but Benicio had disagreed.

Ignacio usually sided with his mother's assessment, but now he knew better. He didn't think she cared any less about him than Benicio, but more than likely, she had been more optimistic about his chances because he was male.

His father shot him a sidelong glance. "What happened to make you think about those days all of a sudden and change your mind about how I limited your activities?"

They stopped near the front of Santana International. "Call it growth. Understanding. Clarity."

"I know show business, and I knew you were not ready for it." His father sighed. "It's easy to be coerced into things you wouldn't want to do because of the glitz and glamour and the money. I knew you loved acting, but as your parent, it was my job to keep you away from harm. There are many young people who left the industry scarred. I didn't want you to suffer like them."

"I understand now, and I'm sorry for being such a little shit back then."

His father smiled. "One day, you'll have your own children, and I expect you to do the same."

"I will, believe me. I'll probably be worse than you, and they'll hate my guts."

"I hope they don't," his father said with a laugh. "Everything with you and Delta is good, yes?"

"We're working through some things, but we're good."

"Hmm. I like her, but no more back-and-forth nonsense. The two of you need to decide if you're going to stay together."

"This time is different. We will."

"I hope so. Let me know how things go with The Cordoba Agency, and if you need me again, you know where I am."

"Thanks."

Benicio patted his arm and lifted the brim of the hat to kiss his temple, the way he used to when he was a kid.

Ignacio watched his father enter the building and then headed toward his car. As he waited to cross the street, he pulled out the card again.

The Cordoba Agency.

He'd give them a call today. He sure hoped they could help.

Chapter Twenty-Six

Ignacio sat in the lobby of The Cordoba Agency's Atlanta office, surprised at how quickly they had worked. He had hired them less than a week ago, and they already had results. Though he shouldn't be surprised, as the research he'd done on them listed their company among the best in the business.

He was especially appreciative of the speedy turnaround because Delta was returning from her trip to New York in two days, and he wanted to give her good news. Before she left, she hadn't been herself. She had moved through the house on autopilot and often stared into space, appearing lost in her thoughts, which meant he sometimes had to repeat himself when they talked. Her energetic personality was muted, and even Maria commented privately to him that Delta was quieter than normal and asked if she was okay. He assured his housekeeper that she was fine, but he knew she wasn't. She wore a mask of composure but was really a woman preparing for a fallout of epic proportions.

Ignacio's feet tapped the floor anxiously as he waited for

the full report. The appointment setter who had called said he'd be meeting with Tyrone, an IT specialist named Raheem, and the head of the company, Cruz.

Finally, a tall, fit woman with short blonde hair approached. By her walk and posture, he suspected she was former military. "They're ready to see you, Mr. Santana. Right this way."

Ignacio followed her down a carpeted hallway to a door at the end, which she cracked open. He entered an office with sleek chrome and glass furniture. Inside, two men sat next to each other in the sitting area on Scandinavian furniture that matched the modern decor. The light-skinned man he recognized as Tyrone, whom he had talked to virtually. The other man was dark-skinned, and Ignacio assumed he was Raheem. Behind the desk was a large Hispanic-looking man.

"Mr. Santana, welcome. I'm Cruz Cordoba."

Ignacio was surprised by exactly how big he was when he stood. He had to be at least five inches over six feet, and the suit he wore barely contained his muscles.

Jesús Cristo, he thought.

"Nice to meet you," he said, shaking Cruz's extended hand.

"Please, join us over here." He gestured toward the other two men, and Ignacio followed. "Would you like anything to drink?"

"They asked me outside when I first arrived, but I'm fine, thank you," Ignacio said, taking a seat across from the others.

Raheem was introduced, and the four men exchanged pleasantries before Cruz, who remained standing behind an armchair, took over the meeting.

"We called you here because we were able to retrieve the video of Miss James, as you requested."

Ignacio felt relief flood his body. "Were there other copies? Were you able to get them all?" he asked anxiously.

"Yes. This is the only copy left." Raheem held out his hand to show a flash drive resting in his palm.

He spoke with such confidence that Ignacio didn't doubt him and breathed easier. "That's good to hear."

"In addition to handing over the video, we need to discuss a troubling discovery." Cruz nodded at Raheem, indicating he should take over.

"We found videos of other women. Dozens of them."

Ignacio's stomach lurched with disgust and shock. "*Dozens*?" he repeated.

"Leo Hargrove is a real scumbag, and apparently, he's been that way for a very long time. Based on metadata in the videos, some of them are older than your partner's video, but there was one filmed as recently as two months ago."

Ignacio muttered a curse. "So he's been violating women all these years, with no intention of stopping."

The three men nodded before Raheem continued. "Like your partner, it's obvious none of these women had any idea they were being filmed. That's part of the thrill for a man like him. Then he can review the tapes whenever he wants and experience the assault all over again."

Nausea climbed up Ignacio's throat as he thought about Leo reviewing the videos of all those women—of Delta—and getting sick pleasure from doing so. He clenched his fists, wanting to tear the man apart piece by piece with his bare hands.

"We're not going to give you the videos of the other women, of course," Raheem continued.

"Of course," Ignacio said. He hadn't expected them to.

"However, before we turn over the video of Miss James, we need to explain something to you. We'd love to see this man get punished for what he's done, but the problem is, if we turn over the evidence we have, these women will have to relive their trauma with no guarantee that Leo will do prison time."

"Mainly because of how the videos were obtained," Tyrone interjected.

"How were they obtained?" Ignacio asked.

"No probable cause, no search warrant, no official law enforcement," Tyrone answered. "Leo is a very powerful man and could walk away from a trial practically unscathed, with no jail time and just a tarnished reputation. Meanwhile, the victims would be re-victimized."

"So we have a request," Raheem said. "We're going to turn over the video of Miss James, and you're going to forget you ever met us or asked for our help."

Ignacio's eyes searched their faces in confusion. Their expressions were blank and emotionless. "I don't understand."

A faint smile curved Raheem's mouth. "We're going to handle the situation from here. Leo Hargrove is filth, and we clean up filth. He won't be allowed to hurt anyone else. We need you to forget you ever asked us to obtain the video for you, and no matter what comes out in the news in the coming days, you keep your mouth shut."

They spoke in calm, low-level voices. Tyrone had his ankle crossed over his knee and his arms stretched across the back of the sofa. Raheem sat calmly, looking at Ignacio with the flash drive resting on his thigh. Cruz remained standing, his large hands gripping the back of the armchair, propping up the weight of the top half of his body.

All three men regarded him with impassive faces—cool and calm, as if there wasn't an undercurrent of violence in Raheem's words. While there was nothing overtly threatening about the men, Ignacio had the distinct impression that he didn't have a choice in the proposed agreement.

"I don't have any problem adhering to those guidelines," he said.

All he cared about was getting the video for Delta. Whatever happened to Leo as a result of his vile actions was none of his concern. Additionally, he was pleased that because he had contacted the agency, the videos of the other women would be destroyed, they'd never have to know the videos existed, and future women would be safe from Leo.

Cruz straightened and shot a glance at the men he worked with. "*Bueno*, that's what we wanted to hear."

Raheem handed the flash drive to Ignacio. "If you like, we can take you to a room where you can review the video in private."

"No, that's not necessary." He wasn't remotely curious to see a crime being committed, but he also didn't want to violate Delta by watching what that monster had done to her when she was little more than a child. "I do have one question. You're confident it's Delta in the video?"

"We have no doubt. We're also certain it's Leo. For a brief moment, his profile is captured on camera, and he talks in the video. We used voice recognition software to help confirm his identity."

Ignacio breathed easier. "Thank you."

Slipping the drive into the inside pocket of his jacket, he left the office. Randall was waiting in the lobby and stood when he stepped off the elevator.

They left the building and walked to the waiting sedan.

Now all he had to do was prepare for Delta's arrival on Thursday.

Chapter Twenty-Seven

Ignacio waited in the doorway as Delta walked slowly toward the front door. She wore her purple coat cinched at the waist, oversized dark sunglasses, and her hair twisted into a loose bun on top of her head.

Behind her, the driver removed her bags from the trunk of the car.

"How was your trip?" he asked.

"Good."

He hated that he couldn't see her eyes.

"I'll take those," he said to the driver, who approached with her luggage in hand.

"Are you sure, sir? I could—"

"It's fine. Thank you." Ignacio took the carry-on and grasped the handle of the rolling suitcase.

"You're welcome, sir."

As the driver returned to the car, Ignacio followed Delta inside and closed the door against the cold. He then took the stairs up to their bedroom.

Their bedroom. He didn't know exactly when he had

begun to think of the room as theirs, but the thought was now automatic. He couldn't imagine staying in the house without her. It was *their* house now. The place where they had become reacquainted and confessed their love for one another. Living together had reminded him of all the characteristics he appreciated about her, as well as revealed new reasons to love her.

Ignacio re-entered the bedroom after placing her luggage in the closet. "We need to talk."

"I know." Delta placed her large leather purse on the trunk at the foot of the bed. "Life is so funny. I don't know what to think. The news didn't offer much information."

"News? Is there something in particular I was supposed to have seen?" Ignacio asked.

"You don't know?"

"Know what?"

Slowly, she removed her sunglasses and placed them on top of the bag. Then she sat on the edge of the bed, her shoulders rounding in an odd display of resignation. "Leo Hargrove is dead."

"Dead?" Ignacio repeated, in genuine shock. *Holy shit.* Had those men from The Cordoba Agency...? "How do you know he's dead?"

"It's all over the news. On the ride from the airport, I read several articles about what happened. A member of his security team found him floating face down in his pool last night. As of now, there doesn't seem to be any foul play, just a freak accident. He'd been drinking with friends, and apparently after everyone left, he must have continued drinking and slipped and fell into the pool. A member of his security was doing his rounds, checking the property before he left, when he found Leo."

Ignacio pulled out his phone, and sure enough, the executive's death was trending online. He did a quick search and skimmed a piece summarizing the news of Leo's passing. Much of what was available at the moment was speculation mingled with accolades about his accomplishments in the music industry.

"I guess I have to wait for the fallout," Delta said quietly.

"What do you mean?"

She let out a small laugh. "Don't you get it? He's dead, and what he did to me will be discovered. Someone will find the video, and what happened to me will come out, and there's nothing I can do about it."

"You're wrong. Everything is going to be fine."

"I want to be optimistic like you are, but I'm a realist. I have to brace myself because it's only a matter of time."

Ignacio sat beside her and took her hand. "Remember when I told you I would take care of everything?"

Her eyebrows lowered over her eyes. "Yes."

He reached into his pocket, removed the flash drive with the video, and handed it to her.

Delta examined the device, turning it over in her hand. "What is this?"

"The video."

Confusion clouded her eyes. "*The* video?"

When Ignacio nodded, she drew in a sharp breath.

"How did you get this?" she whispered. "*Where* did you get it?"

Ignacio didn't want to lie, but he had promised The Cordoba Agency team that he would not divulge his connection to them. This would be the last time he kept vital information from Delta.

"I hired some people to retrieve the video for me, and they confirmed there are no other copies."

"You *hired* people?" Delta asked, suspicion heavy in her voice. "When you said you'd do whatever you had to do..."

"It's not what you think."

"Who are these people, Ignacio?" She dropped her voice lower than before. "Did you have him killed?"

"No, although I did want him dead for what he did to you sixteen years ago and for what he put you through by sending those images and threatening to release the video. I would have gladly killed him myself if I could figure out a way to get away with it, but when I received the drive, Leo was alive. I don't know if the men I hired had anything to do with his death. It could be a coincidence that he happened to die now."

What he said was true. He didn't know anything for certain about whether the agency he hired had anything to do with Leo's death. Maybe he really did just fall into the pool and drown.

"Coincidence," Delta murmured, scrutinizing the drive in her palm. She seemed shocked, as if she couldn't believe she was holding the evidence in her hand. "You're certain this is the last and only copy left?"

"I trust these guys," Ignacio said.

"Who are they?"

"Their identity isn't important. They're professionals and good at what they do." He paused. "They found other videos, Delta. There were other victims."

Her eyes widened in alarm. "No," she said, barely above a whisper.

"He got what he deserved."

"Maybe his death is karma for all the evil he committed. Bastard."

Ignacio placed an arm around her shoulders, and she leaned against him. He kissed the top of her head.

"I can't believe you did this for me," Delta said.

"I would do anything for you."

She didn't speak for a while, continuing to stare at the drive in her hand. "Did you look at the video?" she asked in a small voice.

"No."

"I don't want to look at it, either. I want to destroy it."

"We can do that."

Delta lifted her head and looked into his eyes. "Let's build a fire."

She rose from the bed, and he followed her downstairs and into the backyard, where they built a fire in the fire pit. Ignacio stood back while she stood over the flames.

"Is it really over?" she asked, her voice trembling.

"Yes," he answered.

He wished he could have helped her sooner. If he had known, he would have, and he could have saved her all the years of doubting her talents and avoiding that pig for the sake of her own sanity.

Delta tossed the drive into the fire. It landed with a soft *thunk* on the glowing embers, and the flames popped and hissed. Slowly, the drive blistered under the intense heat, and the casing warped as the flames consumed the evidence.

Head bent, she turned to Ignacio with jerky movements.

"Thank you," she whispered.

He enveloped her in his arms, rubbing his hands up and down her back in a soothing motion as she quietly sobbed her relief into his chest.

Later, as they lay in bed together, Delta propped herself up on her elbow and looked at Ignacio, who was leaning against the headboard with pillows.

"We haven't talked about my trip to New York."

"How did your interviews go?"

"*Extremely* well. The radio interviewers all played a teaser of 'On My Knees' from the album and were very receptive to the sound. They thought it was sexy, the singing was on point, and it had a great beat. The meetings at the label were very productive. I was surprised by how receptive they were to my ideas. They're willing to incorporate my songs into the album, *but* only if I can record them right away, which will give them enough time to mix and master the songs so they can be included."

"So you won't have to push back the album release date?"

"Nope," she said, shaking her head. "The schedule will stay the same, but I will have to work extra hard in the coming weeks—which includes working through the holidays."

"It'll be worth the sacrifice."

"Definitely. They're including my love songs!"

She released a little squeal and bit her lip. For the first time in days, the old spark returned as excitement brightened her pretty brown eyes.

"What are you thinking?" Ignacio asked.

"I feel... free. To celebrate, I'm thinking about dyeing my hair," she said with a laugh.

Ignacio wound a strand of her soft hair around his finger. "What color this time?"

"I'm not sure. I thought about trying a new shade, but I really liked the pink hair and the purple hair I used to have. I can't decide between them."

"I liked the purple phase you went through a few years back," Ignacio said.

"Then I'll go with purple." The smile slowly faded from her face. "I need to have a talk with my father and let him know about the changes, and I need to let him know about a decision I've made. I no longer want him to be my manager, Ignacio. I owe a lot to my parents' guidance, especially my father. If not for him, I wouldn't have the career I have, but..."

In the ambient light of the room, he saw the way her brow wrinkled in consternation.

"You don't owe him your life, Delta."

"I know I don't, but that doesn't make what I'm going to do any easier. You grew up in the entertainment industry, and you've always been wealthy. Your family is drowning in money. I grew up middle class. My mother was a teacher and my father a lawyer before they left their jobs to help me pursue my career as a singer. The money I make has transformed the lives of my entire family. Telling my father I no longer want him involved in my career isn't going to be easy, but I'm ready to have that talk because I need to break free. It's long overdue."

Ignacio rolled onto his side to face her. "That's going to be tough."

"Yeah."

"I'll come with you, so you don't have to do it alone."

She shook her head and gently stroked the stubble on his chin. "Thank you, but you've done so much already."

"And I'm willing to do much more."

She kissed his lips, humming her pleasure. "I need to do this on my own. Can you understand that?"

"I don't like your decision, but yes, I understand. When are you going to talk to him?"

"Tomorrow. The sooner, the better."

"You're sure you don't want me to come with you?"

"I'm positive. I can handle this on my own."

"I'll allow you to handle the dissolution of the management relationship with your father under one condition."

"What's that?"

"You have to move in here permanently with me."

Delta pushed him onto his back and climbed on top of him.

"We had an agreement. Our arrangement was supposed to end when you received funding and I released my first single from the album. I'm releasing my first single next month, which falls within the six-month guidelines."

"That's where you made your mistake," Ignacio said regretfully.

"Oh?"

"You didn't get it in writing." He shrugged. "So now you have to stay. Indefinitely."

"Is there anything I can do to fight this decision?"

"No. Nothing. Sorry."

"You don't sound sorry."

"Because I'm not—not really." He tucked her hair behind her left ear and gazed into her eyes. "So what do you say, *mi amor*? Let's see if we can buy this place and make it our permanent home in Atlanta."

"I love that idea. Because I love this house. And I love you."

Chapter Twenty-Eight

"I'm starving," Vivian said as she wheeled her chair to the dining room table.

"You're always starving," Delta teased, taking a seat across from her.

Her decision to come here and cut off her father hadn't been made lightly. The trip to New York and her success in the meeting made her realize she had become complacent, allowing her father to control much of her career with very little push-back from her. The trip also made her realize she could advocate for herself, and when she found a new manager, she intended to speak up more often so major decisions were more collaborative instead of one person being in control.

Nonetheless, her heart was heavy. Making fun of her sister was a way of fighting the queasiness in her stomach because she knew, after this dinner, her family would be irrevocably broken.

"Whatever. You're only saying that because you survive on a diet of carrot sticks and ice cubes. The rest of us normal folks don't have to worry about our appearance, thank you very much." Vivian grinned across the table at her.

"I'm eating bread today." Delta picked up a roll, broke it in half, and stuffed the bread in her mouth.

Vivian let out an exaggerated gasp. "Whoa."

"I know I didn't see you eat a piece of bread." Edward's deep voice filled every corner of the dining room as he entered, with her mother close behind him.

The smile on Vivian's face died as she looked across the table at her sister. Delta's insides shriveled up. "I had a little piece," she said.

"Good grief, Eddie, she's allowed to have bread every now and again," her mother, Jocelyn, said. Her skin was two shades lighter than Vivian and Delta, and she wore her hair in a curly bob.

"She has promo pictures coming up. She doesn't want to look bloated." Edward sat down and smiled at Delta. "You know I only have your best interests at heart, don't you?"

"I do. Thanks for the reminder." Delta carefully placed the leftover bread on the table. "Are you feeling better?"

"Much better, thanks. Doctor said it was acid reflux. He recommended antacids and gave a list of foods to cut back on. See, we all have to cut back if it's in our best interest. How did things go in New York? I want to hear all about your interviews and meetings," her father said.

As dinner was served, Delta launched into a recounting of her time in New York, where she had been accompanied by her publicist and an assistant. She explained that her interviews had gone well, and the radio DJs liked the sample of "On My Knees," the first single to be released from the album.

"That's good. Your promotional gigs for next week were confirmed today. In a couple of days, I should have the schedule for after the new year. You know the drill. Things are going to be crazy leading up to the release of the first single off the album, which will be crazier than normal because of the publicity surrounding your relationship with Ignacio."

"Actually, I wanted to talk to you about the album," Delta said, slicing into her grilled chicken breast. She had steamed vegetables on the side, while her family was eating roasted chicken, mashed potatoes, and brown sugar-glazed carrots.

"What did you want to talk about?"

"My first single won't actually be 'On My Knees.' It's going to be 'I Don't Miss You.'"

Edward's knife and fork hovered above his plate. "What song is that? I don't remember any of your songs having that title."

"It's a song I wrote. I recorded a demo with a few of my own songs, and while I was in New York I shared the performance with people at the label."

"Sweetheart," Edward said with a condescending laugh, "the record label is investing a lot of money in you and has already decided which songs will be included on the album and in which order they'll be released. You can't go making changes all willy-nilly. Who did you talk to?"

"Chase, in A&R. He approved the changes." She saw the shift in her father's composure.

"I see."

He couldn't argue with her answer. Chase was in charge of the album's creative direction, and his approval meant the changes were a done deal.

"You'll have to go back in the studio?" Edward asked.

"Yes. The timeline is tight, but Chase said if I do my part to have the recordings completed on time, they can be included on the album."

"Why didn't you discuss this with me before you went to see him?"

"Because I knew you'd try to talk me out of it."

An uneasy silence permeated the room. Vivian and Jocelyn watched Delta and her father's conversation with their eyes bouncing back and forth like spectators watching a tennis match.

"I don't know what's going on with you, Delta. The other day I asked about you and Ignacio, and the way you talked about him—well, you sounded like a woman in a real relationship, not a fake one. Now this. Is he putting ideas in your head?"

"I'm an adult. Despite what you believe, I can think for myself."

"Don't be disrespectful to your father," Jocelyn admonished.

"You want me to have more respect for him?"

"*He is your father.*"

Delta felt as if her chest was caving in, and suddenly she no longer cared about propriety and respect and manners and sparing the feelings of her parents. She was a grown woman, and it was time to prioritize her happiness and her peace. Time for *them* to respect *her*.

"And you're my mother." She blew out a breath. "So why didn't you protect me?"

"What are you talking about?" Edward demanded in a sharp voice.

The weight of emotion threatened to overcome her, but this time she wouldn't allow the heavy load to crush her. One hand tightened into a fist beside her plate.

"Why did you leave me with Leo?" Delta asked.

Jocelyn gasped, bringing a hand to her throat.

Delta lifted her gaze to her father. "I'm sure you saw that he died."

He didn't move, as if he had been turned into stone.

"I keep going over it again and again in my head, and I can't reconcile what you did," Delta continued.

"W-we didn't do anything," Edward said.

"That's the problem! You did nothing, and you knew. You *knew*. So why didn't you *protect me!*" She slammed her fist on the table and screamed the last sentence, shaking with anger and hurt.

Carefully putting down his silverware, Edward swallowed. "I…" He paused, shook his head, and then continued. "Sometimes… sometimes sacrifices have to be made."

"Sacrifices?" Delta repeated, incredulous.

"Do you think I wanted that for you? Of course I didn't, but look at everything you have now. You're past the incident."

"I'm not. I'm dealing with the remnants of what happened even now. I'm going to be better because he's gone, but for the longest time, I felt alone because of what happened to me."

"What are you guys talking about?" Vivian asked.

Edward's eyes pleaded with her not to say, but Delta was beyond caring. The truth needed to come out.

"When I was sixteen, Mom and Dad left me alone with Leo Hargrove for a weekend so he could do whatever he wanted."

"That's not why we left you there! He was supposed to help you," Edward said.

Her sister's eyes widened in horror. "D, what do you mean? Are you saying…?"

Delta nodded. "Yeah," she said in a thick voice.

Vivian stared at her father, then her mother, whose head was bent in shame, and then back at her father again. "Is this a joke? What's going on right now?"

"It's not a joke." Delta used her napkin to dab at the single tear that streamed out the corner of her right eye.

Edward lifted his watery eyes to Delta. "If you needed help, you could have gone back to the treatment center."

"I shouldn't have needed a goddamn treatment center in the first place. Don't you understand that?"

"We had a lot of bills. Your sister—"

"Don't you dare bring Viv into this!" Delta snapped.

"All right, you're clearly upset," Edward said in a placating voice. "We should probably discuss this in private. Why don't we table this conversation until later?"

"We're not going to table anything, we're not delaying the conversation, and we're not going anywhere else to talk. I came here for a very specific reason today, to tell you that I'm done. All my life, I've done things your way, and I'm ready to do things my way."

"What does that mean?" Her mother's voice was a jarring surprise as she joined the conversation.

"It means, Mom, that I no longer want Dad to be my manager. I've consulted an attorney, and I'm hereby giving you verbal notice that I'm ending our work relationship. A more formal dissolution of our arrangement will come later." Edward opened his mouth to speak, but she cut him off. "If you try to fight me, I will leak what you allowed to happen."

She was bluffing, but he didn't know that and quickly shut his mouth. She knew him so well, she wasn't the least bit surprised he was about to make an argument in an effort to remain her manager.

"Mom, your advisory role is also terminated. I'll work up a severance package for both of you. You're smart people. I'm sure you can figure out how to make the money last. I'm also selling the house, and I'm permanently moving in with Ignacio, which means you'll have to leave here at some point."

"Delta, we're your family. Your parents," her mother said.

She closed her eyes and took a deep breath, letting it out

slowly past her lips. When she opened her eyes again, she looked directly across the table at her sister and smiled.

"Viv, I want you to come with me. I talked to Ignacio about it this morning, and we want you to live with us."

"Are you sure?" Vivian asked, sounding surprised.

"Yes, I'm sure. We both are."

"Somehow, this man has convinced you to turn your back on your family and risk tanking your career. You need guidance. This is what I was afraid of when you were younger. He has too much influence over you," Edward said.

"No, *you* had too much influence over me, and that ends today. We're still family, but you will no longer be a part of my business and use it to run my life." Delta pushed back her chair. "My lawyer will be in touch."

She headed toward the door, abruptly stopped, and returned to the table. She picked up the half-eaten roll, slathered it with butter, and stuffed it in her mouth while locking eyes with her father.

She caught Vivian's proud smile before she stalked out of the dining room, feeling as if she had conquered the world.

Chapter Twenty-Nine

As Delta stirred beneath the thick duvet, sunlight streamed through the window and cast a golden glow over the room. She was in bed alone on Christmas morning. Ignacio had probably gone on his morning run, which he rarely missed. His discipline was admirable.

She, however, intended to take full advantage of this day off. Between recording the additional songs for the album and attending promotional events, she had a packed schedule.

She stretched lazily and blinked sleep from her eyes, recalling her conversation with Ignacio when she returned from seeing her family a few days ago. He had been in the kitchen eating dinner.

Ignacio perked up when he saw her. "You're back earlier than expected. How did the conversation with your father go?"

Seeking comfort, she walked over and slid between his thighs. One of his arms curled around her waist, anchoring her to him.

"It was difficult, but our conversation went better than I thought it would. No real drama to speak of."

Ignacio's eyebrows lifted in mild surprise. "Shocking."

"I might have also threatened to let the world know what he allowed."

"Ahh, I see how that could make him willing to accept your plans. How do you feel?"

Delta rested her hands on his shoulders. "It'll take some getting used to. My father has been in control of my career since I was a kid."

"But you're okay?" His eyes searched hers.

"I will be."

He studied her for a moment and then nodded, trusting her words. "What did Vivian say when you proposed moving in?"

She smiled. "She wants to move in with us." Having her sister with her was important, and she was happy Vivian accepted the invitation. She and her sister could continue to look out for each other. Winding her arms around Ignacio's neck, Delta held his gaze. "You know what I need right now?"

He smirked and teasingly pumped his hips twice against hers.

She giggled. "Not that."

"Oh, my mistake." His grin was filled with pure mischief. "What did you have in mind?"

"A nice warm bath."

Slowly, he traced circles along her lower back. "Excellent idea. Take your time to relax and enjoy your bath. Later, when you're ready, tell me everything that happened."

After a relaxing bath filled with lavender crystals, Delta recounted her conversation with her father in detail, and then they cuddled in the living room and watched TV.

Yawning, she rolled out of bed and padded into the bathroom. She went through her morning routine and then brushed her hair into a sleek ponytail. She added earrings and dressed in dark jeans and a cashmere sweater.

She and Ignacio were going to exchange gifts and then pick up Vivian so she could join them at his family's place. They had purchased gifts for his nieces and nephews and for the Dirty Santa game they were going to play after everyone ate lunch together.

Her parents had flown to Mexico for a two-week getaway. She assumed they wanted to escape after the confrontation at the house. She still felt a bit of guilt because she'd fired her father but knew the decision would be better for her in the long run.

Delta went downstairs to the kitchen. While making coffee using Ignacio's espresso machine, she heard the distant sound of the front door opening and closing as he returned from his run. Since Maria had gone to spend Christmas with her family, they were on their own for meals, so she whipped up a batch of cinnamon-cranberry muffins. That way, they'd have something to eat before lunch at his mother's estate.

She hummed as she worked and realized she was happy—in a way she hadn't been in a long time. She wasn't just happy, she was blissful.

She stopped stirring the muffins.

Blissful.

As an idea came to her, she began humming again.

By the time she was taking the muffins out of the oven, Ignacio entered the kitchen, impossibly handsome in a black long-sleeved shirt and black jeans. The scent of his shower lingered on his skin—a clean, pine scent that was undeniably masculine. The crisp bite of his woodsy cologne mingled with hints of fresh soap and made her want to slip her fingers under his clothes and press her nose to his chest to breathe him in.

"Good morning, Merry Christmas," he said, drawing in a deep breath. "Smells good in here."

"Merry Christmas! We have coffee and muffins for breakfast," Delta announced, placing the hot pan on a silicone trivet.

Ignacio came closer and peered at the muffins. "You've been busy."

"Mhmm. Try this." Delta handed him a cup of coffee and waited.

He took a sip, and his eyebrows lifted in surprise. "Mmm. You finally learned to make coffee the way I like."

"And it only took seven billion tries because you're so particular."

Ignacio chuckled. "One of these days, your mouth is going to get you into trouble. Mark my words." He playfully smacked her bottom.

"Ouch." Pretending he hurt her, Delta rubbed her butt. "I have something to tell you."

"What?" Ignacio carefully removed a muffin from the hot pan.

"I decided on a name for the album."

"I thought you already had a name."

"I did, but I like this one better. I'm going to run it by A&R, but they should be fine with it."

"What's the new title?" He bit into the muffin. "Damn, this is good."

"Thank you. The new title is *Blissful*."

He seemed to consider the title. "I like it."

"I think it perfectly sums up the sense of complete happiness and joy I feel. No matter what happens in the future, good or bad, I know this is the album I wanted to create—*my* artistic vision. I have inner peace because I know the pain from my past is finally truly behind me. And then there's you."

"Me?"

"Yes, you. You've been supportive and loving, and being

with you has changed me for the better. I am blissfully happy with you, Mr. Santana."

"You've changed me too. I used to think I was happy, but those emotions don't compare to how I feel right now, with you. I hated the idea of being in a fake relationship with you, but it turned out to be a good idea."

"I agree. The best idea." She smiled at him. "So, what time are we leaving to pick up Viv?"

"We can go right after we open our gifts, unless you have something else you need to do. Are all the gifts wrapped?"

Delta nodded. "I wrapped the Dirty Santa gifts last night. They're under the tree with the others."

"Then we don't have anything else to do except open our gifts, load up your car, and head out."

Since they were picking up Vivian, they were going to use Delta's SUV.

"I'll call Viv when we're on our way so she can tell her attendant."

When they picked up her sister today, she was going to stay with them through the holidays and move in all her belongings after the New Year, when Delta put her house on the market.

"I'm ready to open gifts. Let's go." Delta grabbed her coffee and a muffin and led the way into the living room, the only space decorated for Christmas. Next year she intended to do more, but with the holiday fast approaching, she hadn't had much time to transform the house.

A lush fir stood in a corner of the living room, adorned with gold and silver ornaments, white ribbon, and twinkling lights, gifts nestled underneath. She had draped a garland of pine and holly across the fireplace mantel and attached three stockings with the initials V, I, and D. The rest of the decor included crystal reindeer and a silver tray with candles, cinnamon sticks, and dried oranges. Red and gold pillows had replaced the usual ones on the chairs, and a throw with *Merry Christmas* on it was draped over the arm of the sofa.

Ignacio and Delta settled on the floor, and she handed him his gift.

"Here you go."

Ignacio shook the box. "What is this?"

"Open it!" She grinned, barely able to contain her excitement.

He tore off the paper and paused when he saw the Patek Philippe name on the box. He shot a glance at her and then finished opening his gift. Inside was a watch with an oversized face and black band.

"It's vintage, from 1943. I have the paperwork to confirm its authenticity."

"Sweetheart, I love it."

Ignacio placed a hand at the back of her neck and pulled her in for a kiss. When their mouths touched, his lips were warm and sure against hers, and she melted into him, cupping his jaw. This was the exact reaction she had been hoping for. Ignacio had been so good to her, she had wanted to give him something special and knew he would appreciate the timepiece from one of his favorite brands.

"Of course I'm wearing this today." He fastened the watch around his wrist. "All right. Your turn." He handed her a large bag covered with reindeer images.

"What could this be...?" Delta sang, removing the tissue paper. She gasped when she saw the two boxes in unmistakable Hermès orange.

"Baby..." She opened the first box and gasped again. "You bought me the Birkin?" The gold matte crocodile Birkin cost over six figures.

"Of course," Ignacio said, looking very pleased with himself.

Delta hugged the bag and kissed it. "I love it." She opened the next box, which contained calfskin Hermès sandals. "I love these too! I can't wait until the weather warms up so I can wear them. Thank you, baby!"

She flung herself at Ignacio and gave him an appreciative kiss.

Ignacio frowned. "Were those the only two gifts in the bag?" he asked.

"Yeah," Delta answered.

"There should have been another box. Maybe it fell out. Check under the tree."

"Another present? You're spoiling me." She hopped up and glanced under the tree, moving two gifts out of the way in her search. "I don't see anything."

"Keep looking. Maybe it's behind the tree."

Though she doubted it could have fallen back there, she did as he asked. "Ignacio, I don't see—"

"Here it is."

She turned, and her breath caught. Ignacio was down on one knee holding a small velvet box in his hand. Her heart pounded in her ears as he slowly opened the box and revealed a ring with a square stone in a breathtaking green color, surrounded by white diamonds.

"It's a green diamond, extremely rare," Ignacio explained, his voice steady but laced with emotion. "When I told my mother I wanted to marry you, she let me have the ring. It's a family heirloom. I should have returned it to her when you and I never got engaged, but I held onto it. I don't know why. Maybe because I was hoping, wishing, that someday you'd wear it. Or maybe because I didn't want anyone else to have it. I always thought of this ring as yours."

Delta covered her mouth with one hand, her eyes filling with tears.

"I love you so much. You make me laugh, I can share my dreams with you—my ups and downs. I can just be myself. I want to know that you'll be mine forever. Will you marry me, Delta?"

A breathless laugh escaped her throat. "Are you serious?"

"I've never been more serious in my life."

"Yes. Of course, yes!"

A relieved smile spread across Ignacio's face as he slid the ring onto her finger. Perfect fit. She threw herself into his arms, knocking him backward onto the floor.

She pressed kisses all over his face as he laughed, holding her tightly.

Finally, Delta pulled back. "This is the best Christmas present I could ever have. I love you."

They kissed tenderly, which slowly turned into something more, and Ignacio groaned.

"We have to go. We need to pick up Vivian, and my family's expecting us."

"We have a little time," she whispered, undoing his belt.

A lazy smile touched his lips. "I like the way you think." He pulled her down for another sweet kiss.

They undressed in a rush, whispering and laughing, enjoying each other. Delta climbed on top of Ignacio and took him in her mouth, stretching her lips around his rigid length. This was her man, and she wanted to make him feel good.

She swirled her tongue around the tip of his dick, immensely satisfied by the groans that were torn from his chest. He guided her movements with a hand on her head, gently pumping so he slid back and forth in her mouth.

Grabbing her hair, Ignacio lifted her head from his body. "Get on top of me," he commanded.

Delta did as he asked and sank onto his hard flesh, sighing as waves of pleasure coursed through her body. She rode him slowly, feeling his hands slide up her waist to her heavy breasts—kneading and massaging, then teasing and tweaking her hard nipples.

Right as she started to come, he stiffened and came too. She tossed her head back and indulged in the passion exploding in her loins. She ground her pelvis against his, mouth open, gasping and riding while he held her hips and grunted through the throes of ecstasy.

She finally collapsed on top of him, completely spent, her body turned to liquid and her racing heart matching the rapid beating of his in his chest.

"I will never let you go again," Ignacio breathed against her neck.

Delta wanted to speak but was too overwhelmed by emotion. She lost track of how long they stayed in the same position, their damp bodies locked together as one—savoring the moment and each other before they had to share the news of their engagement with the rest of the world.

Epilogue

Standing in the crowded arena, Ignacio watched Delta in awe. He could have stood on the side of the stage but preferred being in front with the audience, where he could experience the full effect of her performance.

During the concert, she had gone through multiple costume changes, but at the moment she wore a sparkling white gown and her purple hair in an elegant updo. With the spotlight on her, and the rest of the stage in darkness, she sang the biggest hit from her latest album—"I Don't Miss You." Although she had been hesitant to share the deeply personal song, it resonated with fans.

He had been to almost all her shows during the tour, yet every single time he was blown away by her stage presence and talent. Vivian, seated beside him, squeezed his hand. He glanced at her, and they both beamed with pride.

Blissful was a critical and commercial success, exceeding everyone's expectations by reaching the top of the Billboard charts and garnering three number-one hits for the first time in Delta's career. "Unworthy" and "Bad Behavior," both written by her, were the other two songs that had climbed to the top of the charts. Music journalists praised Delta's evolution as an artist, using words like "masterpiece" and commending her for the "raw honesty" in her lyrics.

As her voice soared over the crowd in the heartrending song, the green stone on her finger caught the light as her hand gripped the microphone. After eleven long years, the heirloom ring was finally in its rightful place. More than an engagement ring, it was a symbol of defiance and forgiveness, a reminder that love, once interrupted, could be reborn in the light of understanding.

Don't want to see you
Don't want to hear you
I'm at my limit
No, I don't miss you
But I do wish you
Only the best

Don't dream about you
Don't think about you
Not on my mind
You're not important
Thank God it's over
I can move on
I only want to forget about you, and the memories

(*Chorus*)
I don't miss you
Don't miss the way that you say my name
I don't miss, I don't miss, I don't miss you
See you again I might go insane
I don't miss, I don't miss, I don't miss you

My friends won't listen
They keep insisting
That I'm still in love
I'm Aphrodite
There's no one like me
And I have had enough

My hands are shaking
My heart is aching
I can't explain it
I really hate it
I hate your gray eyes
I hate your warm smile
I can't stop screaming
I only want to forget about you, and the memories

(Chorus)
I don't miss you
Don't miss the way that you say my name
I don't miss, I don't miss, I don't miss you
See you again I might go insane
I don't miss, I don't miss, I don't miss you

I don't long to hear your laugh
I feel free, I'm free at last
I can finally sleep through the night (I don't miss, I don't miss)
I don't long to hear your laugh
I feel free, I'm free at last
I can finally sleep through the night (I don't miss, I don't miss)

(Chorus)
I don't miss you
Don't miss the way that you say my name

I don't miss, I don't miss, I don't miss you
See you again I might go insane
I don't miss, I don't miss, I don't miss you

I don't long to hear your laugh
I feel free, I'm free at last
I can finally sleep through the night (I don't miss, I don't miss)
I don't long to hear your laugh
I feel free, I'm free at last
I can finally sleep through the night (I don't miss, I don't miss)

Ain't a dream, it ain't a wish
Not a damn thing that I miss
Not a damn thing that I miss
(I don't miss, I don't miss, I don't miss you)
I won't beg and I won't plead
I won't drop down on my knees
Baby, won't you please set me free
(I still love, I still love, I still love you)

When the song ended, the crowd—who had joined in on the final chords with Delta—erupted into deafening screams and thunderous applause. Since she ended each show with "I Don't Miss You," they knew the night was coming to an end.

She blew kisses to the audience. "I love you, Miami!" she shouted into the microphone, her voice brimming with energy.

The lights behind her flared to life and illuminated the band. Then her ten dancers burst onto the stage, grinning and waving. One by one, Delta called their names, giving each of them a moment to soak in the roaring applause.

Finally, she said, "Good night, Miami! Thank you! Thank you so much!"

As the arena lights slowly brightened so the audience could leave, Ignacio and Vivian headed off the floor.

"Time for the backstage dash," he remarked.

She laughed, the sound reminding him very much of Delta's bubbly laugh.

"Lead the way, future brother-in-law."

They made their way backstage where the crew members, dancers, band, and security had crowded into the Green Room, filling it with laughter and excited conversation. Ignacio and Vivian slipped in behind them and hovered near the back.

Delta stood in the center of the room, her face glowing, her stage outfit sparkling against her chestnut skin. Hands clasped together, she did what she always did after each show—thanked everyone for making the night a success. As she spoke, she turned in a slow circle to make eye contact with each person, her gratitude sincere and unwavering.

As she wrapped up, she said, "Two more nights, and then we get off this crazy ride."

They laughed.

"But it's been a blast," her drummer hollered.

She grinned. "Yes, it has. Well, we hit the road early tomorrow, so let's—"

"Excuse me." Ignacio spoke up.

Everyone turned to look at him.

"Before you all leave, I have something to say."

"Uh, okay." Delta eyed him with confusion.

Everyone knew he was her fiancé, but this was the first time Ignacio had spoken in front of the whole group.

"I'll be right back," he said, hurrying from the room.

When he returned, he walked in slowly, wheeling in a huge rectangular cake covered in buttercream frosting, with candles shaped like the number thirty-three flickering on top. The crowd parted to let him through, and Delta's mouth fell open in surprise. Almost everyone there knew about the plan and had kept his secret.

At Ignacio's cue, the room burst into song.

"Happy birthday to you..."

Standing before her, he sang right along with them. They finished with, "Happy birthday dear Delta... happy birthday to you!"

"And many more!" Vivian added.

The entire room burst into laughter. Seconds later, they were all silent.

"Make a wish, *mi amor*," Ignacio whispered.

"I already have everything I want," she said softly, her gaze never leaving his face.

"Then make a wish for the future," Ignacio encouraged.

He knew what he looked forward to—getting married, having kids, celebrating each other's future successes, and spending their lives together.

Delta closed her eyes, and when she opened them, she blew out the flames. The group cheered, and she clasped Ignacio's face and gave him a quick kiss. "Thank you," she whispered.

"Aww," the group said.

"You guys, stop," Delta said, wiping her lipstick from his mouth with her thumb.

Ignacio stole another kiss from the corner of her mouth before turning to the group. "Who wants cake?"

Raucous cheering filled the room. An assistant wheeled in a smaller tray with plates, champagne, glasses, and utensils.

Ignacio cut a hunk of cake for the birthday girl and sat on the leather sofa with her curled up beside him. The Green Room hummed with celebration, warm laughter, and champagne bubbles. The entire team had to get on the road early tomorrow, but for now, they were going to enjoy spending time together.

"This is so good," Delta said, sighing as she cut into the moist dessert with her fork.

Across the room, the dancers playfully recreated their choreography from one of her up-tempo songs, and the bassist, Marcus, had everyone in stitches with his impression of their stern-faced sound engineer. Vivian watched the shenanigans from her wheelchair, her face bright with joy as she chatted with one of the backup singers.

"I don't think I've ever been happier," Delta said huskily. Her eyes met his, filled with contentment.

Ignacio's heart swelled as he gazed at her. "Me either. And just think, this is only the beginning."

A beautiful smile stretched across her lips. Unable to help himself, he leaned in, his hand cupping the back of her head as he pressed his lips against hers. The kiss was soft, tender, and a promise of all the tomorrows stretching before them.

Someone whistled playfully in their direction, and Delta laughed against his mouth. Settling more comfortably against him, she rested her head on his shoulder.

After the last show, Ignacio had an additional birthday surprise. He planned to whisk her away to Isla Barú, south of Cartagena, Colombia, where he had rented a beachfront villa with a private pool. They would be there for a week before they had to return to their demanding lives.

He planted a soft kiss on her forehead.

The pain and darkness of the past were long gone. All he saw was a bright, happy future—with the woman he loved.

Also by Delaney Diamond

More from the Family Ties series!

Audra - The Prequel (Family Ties #0)

Thanks to an unexpected pregnancy, they both realize that some risks are worth taking—especially when love is at stake.

Ethan (Family Ties #1)

After seven years together, one night, Skye broaches the subject of marriage and learns the devastating truth. Ethan has no intention of marrying her.

Monica (Family Ties #2)

Andre is engaged to marry the daughter of the man who gave him a chance when no one else would, but seeing Monica causes old feelings to resurface and calls his plans into question.

Audra (Family Ties #3)

When Audra asks for a divorce, she and Damon are forced to face the truth about their marriage. Can they rekindle the fire in the relationship... before it's too late?

Bruno (Family Ties #4)

When Bruno hires a matchmaking service to find him a wife, sparks fly between him and the matchmaker, blurring the lines between love and professionalism.

Ignacio (Family Ties #5)

A fake romance could catapult the careers of actor Ignacio Santana and R&B singer Delta James to higher levels—or reignite heartbreak they never recover from.

***

More family series are available!

Visit my Books page at delaneydiamond.com to learn about all my books and the

Johnson Family

Brooks Family

Hawthorne Family

Read more stories about The Cordoba Agency cleaning up the filth in the world in The Cordoba Agency romantic suspense series.

Before Tyrone Evers joined The Cordoba Agency, he was a police detective in Atlanta investigating a scary break-in at the home of billionaire heiress Ella Brooks. Find out how they fell in love in Do Over.

***

Audiobook samples and free short stories available at www.delaneydiamond.com.

About the Author

Delaney Diamond is the USA Today Bestselling Author of sensual, passionate romance novels. Originally from the U.S. Virgin Islands, she now lives in Atlanta, Georgia. She reads romance novels, mysteries, thrillers, and a fair amount of nonfiction. When she's not busy reading or writing, she's in the kitchen trying out new recipes, dining at one of her favorite restaurants, or traveling to an interesting locale.

Enjoy free reads on her website. Join her mailing list to get sneak peeks, notices of sale prices, and find out about new releases.

Join her mailing list
www.delaneydiamond.com

facebook.com/DelaneyDiamond
instagram.com/delaneydiamondbooks
x.com/DelaneyDiamond
pinterest.com/delaneydiamond

www.ingramcontent.com/pod-product-compliance
Lightning Source LLC
Chambersburg PA
CBHW071312250626
47159CB00004B/1400

9781946302885